THE FIXER

NEW WAVE NEWSROOM

JENNY HOLIDAY

The Fixer originally appeared in *'80s Mix Tape*, an anthology published by Pink Kayak Press.

Edited by Gwen Hayes. Copy edited by Polly Watson. Formatting and cover design by Zack Taylor. Cover photo by alla_iatsun via Deposit Photos.

First edition, September 13, 2016

ISBN 978-0-9950927-0-9

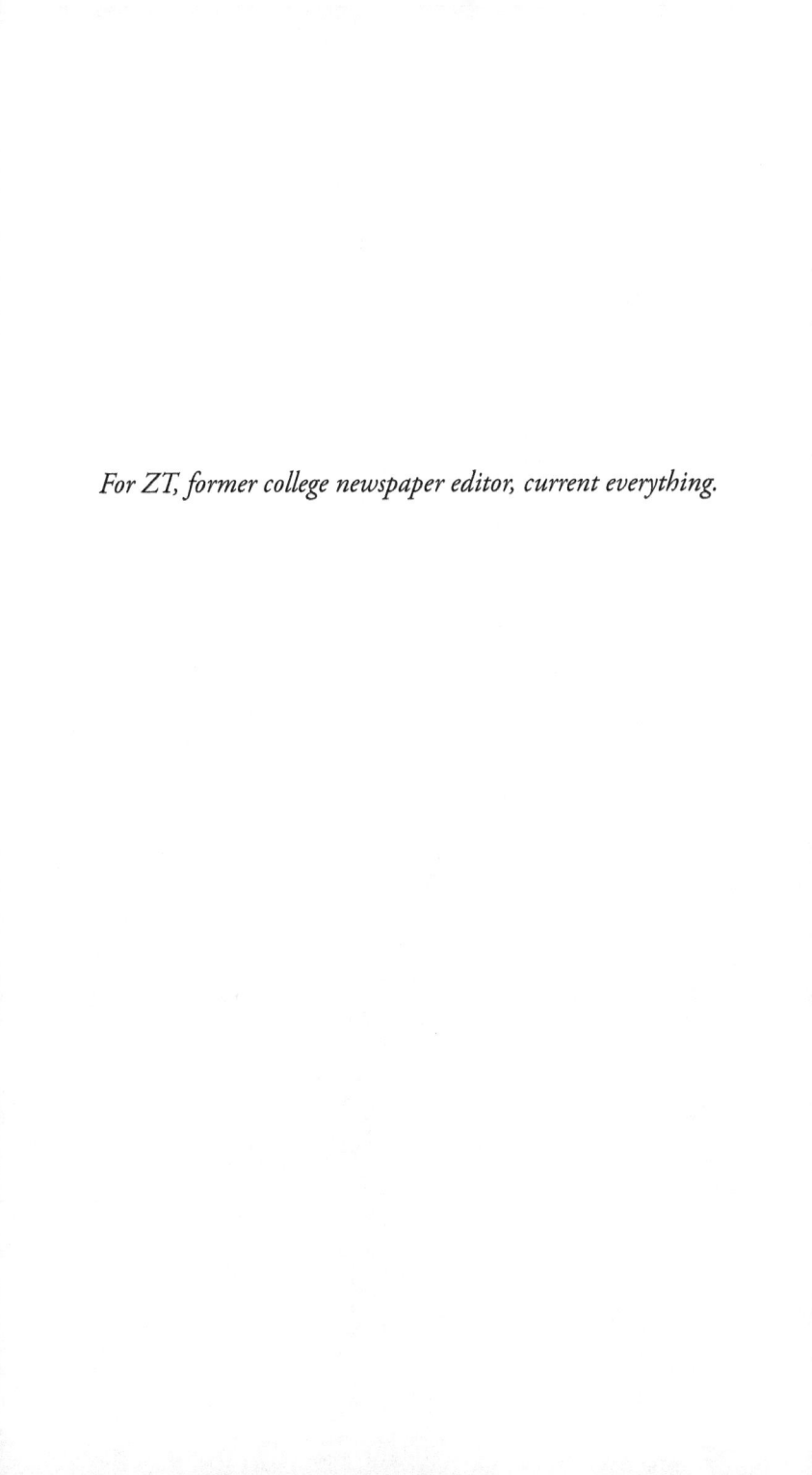

For ZT, former college newspaper editor, current everything.

CHAPTER ONE

Spring 1983

JENNY

I am going to save the art building.
I am going to save the art building.
I am going to save the art building.

I let the words become a mantra, encouraging them to spiral through my mind, hoping that if I whispered them enough times as I trudged across campus to the newspaper office, I might actually be able to do it.

Because God knew, the art building wasn't going to save itself.

You know what else wasn't going to save the art building? An impassioned series of editorials in the student newspaper. Oh, those meticulously researched arguments delving into the history of the Gothic Revival beauty that had housed Allenhurst College's budding artists for more than a hundred years! It killed me, but they weren't working.

It wasn't like I was so idealistic and/or naïve that I thought I could single-handedly make the administration reverse its demolition decision with the power of my words. But I had kind of thought that the articles would bring the issue to the forefront of campus politics. Maybe just enough that people would come to the sit-in I had organized in the president's office last week.

Nope. It had been just me and my roommate Vanessa and a handful of the *Allenhurst Examiner* staff who, frankly, were jockeying for the editor-in-chief job that would fall vacant when I graduated this spring. We tried to take up a lot of space in the president's suite of offices, but mostly his staff just walked awkwardly around us until someone called the campus cops and Officer Artie talked me into closing up shop. "Come on, Jenny," he'd said. (Officer Artie knew me well.) "You can't save everything." (But obviously not well enough.)

So, okay. It was time for Plan B.

I just didn't know what that was yet.

"Morning, you guys," I said as I dumped my stuff on my desk in the newsroom. We had an editorial meeting this morning, so pretty much everyone was in.

Vanessa, the production coordinator—and my room-mate—flashed me a tired smile from the large worktable in the center of the space. The paper came out twice a week, and Nessa was in charge of the pasteups. That meant late nights before we went to press for our Tuesday and Thursday editions.

Occasionally, she pulled all-nighters in the office, though in my two years as editor, I had made it a mission to streamline operations so that everything was more predictable. You couldn't control the news, of course, but processes could always be tweaked and made more efficient. There was always room for improvement. The Columbia University Graduate School of Journalism wasn't just looking for good writers: they were looking for people with vision to lead newsrooms.

So when Vanessa called last night to say she wouldn't be coming back to our room because the mechanicals had arrived late, I only pretended to believe her. If she really had been working on pasteups late into the night, we both knew I would have been there with her.

Which meant we both knew she had spent the night with her loser boyfriend, Royce. It almost made me shudder. But, hey, as Nessa had pointed out several times in recent (increasingly tense) weeks, I was not her mother.

If only the college administration would turn its attention to getting rid of Royce Waldorf with the same vehemence with which it was attempting to destroy the art building. Unlike Royce Waldorf, the art building had never done anything to hurt anyone.

But one cause at a time.

I shed my jacket and moved over to the dusty blackboard on which my section editors had already scrawled their proposed lineups for next Tuesday's paper.

"What's this?" I said, trying to keep my tone casual as I pointed at an item that said, "Editorial: National Drinking Age Act—anti."

No one answered. No one met my eye.

"Seriously? You're proposing an editorial defending the rights of teenagers to drink?" I wasn't a Pollyanna—at least not a *total* Pollyanna—but really? That's what they thought was important?

"It's not about drinking, Jen," said Beth, a freshman reporter who was pretty much my smartest staff member. I respected the heck out of her despite her relative inexperience. "It's about civil liberties, the nanny state."

No one else said anything, but I knew what they were thinking. We'd already devoted three editorials to the art building. That was a lot of real estate for one topic. But if I could save the building with the newspaper, my chances of getting into Columbia for grad school would skyrocket. Heck, they'd probably give me a prestigious fellowship.

But, I reminded myself, great editors didn't use their papers to further their own agendas. And the drinking-age editorial was topical and just controversial enough that it would get people talking. I sighed, the fight leaving me. "All right."

"Maybe we can think of something else for the art building," Nessa, ever the people pleaser, said. "An editorial cartoon, maybe?"

"Or maybe you need to think outside the confines of campus," our photographer, Tony, suggested. "Are there any celebrities you could get on board with your cause?"

It wasn't a bad idea. "Are there any alumni who have gone on to be successful artists?" I wondered aloud.

"Emmanuel Curry," said Tony, who was minoring in art.

"Never heard of him. But that doesn't mean anything. I'm not much into art."

"Just art *buildings*," Nessa teased. "I've heard of Emmanuel Curry. I saw some of his stuff at the Met last summer when I was in New York."

I *had* heard of the Metropolitan Museum of Art. Hmm.

"Well, good luck with Curry," said Dawn, our gossip columnist and occasional entertainment writer. "He supposedly never does media. I've been trying to get him to agree to a profile for the entire time I've been on staff."

All eyes swung to Dawn, whose column was our most popular offering, much to my chagrin. She'd built kind of a cult brand on campus with Dish with Dawn. I was surprised to learn that she'd been chasing someone like Curry for a serious profile. But maybe I shouldn't have been, because her social connections had yielded a huge story for us last year, when she'd reported on a football player who date-raped a bunch of freshman girls.

"Anyway," she went on, filing her nails and oblivious to the collective bewilderment in the room, "he never replies to my letters, and his agent keeps saying no." She stared into space and sighed. "It would be so gnarly if we could just get him. You always see him in those nightlife pictures at Danceteria with Madonna and New Order and stuff." She sniffed. "Though I have to say, he dresses atrociously."

Ah, that made more sense. The fact that Curry was hanging out with Madonna explained Dawn's interest in him.

"What about that Matthew Townsend kid?" Tony said. "They say he's some kind of prodigy. Like, the art department is losing their shit over him, he's supposedly such a phenom. Dawn is right about Curry—he has a reputation for being standoffish—but somehow the art department managed to get him to agree to mentor Townsend. All the majors have to have a mentor to advise them on their senior portfolio."

"Matthew Townsend." I let the name roll off my tongue slowly, considering.

A "prodigy" art major with a pipeline to a famous alum?

I had found Plan B.

MATTHEW

There were two more messages taped to my door when I got back early that morning.

"Jenny Fields—867-5309," said the first one.

The second: "Call Jenny. IMPORTANT. 867-5309."

This chick didn't know how to take a hint, apparently. She'd called yesterday, too. Jenny, whoever she was, could eat my shorts. If it wasn't Curry or the registrar's office calling about a bounced tuition check or some shit, I didn't want to talk. Not that I *wanted* to talk to Curry or the registrar's office. But they were necessary evils, and so for them—and only them—I would drag my ass to the pay phone in the common room. I didn't have time to dick around. I had four courses and a job, which wasn't anything new. But this semester I also had a senior portfolio I seemed maddeningly incapable of producing to Curry's ridiculous standards—and I wasn't going to graduate without it.

So, yeah, unlike the rest of the rich dweebs at this school, I could not afford to waste time chatting on the phone.

So then why the fuck had I gone out again last night? Did I *want* to flunk out? To spend the rest of my life flipping burgers? Was eighteen hours a week for the past three-plus years not enough burger flipping to last a lifetime?

I dumped my backpack on my bed, and the remorse came flooding in as it always did once I was back in my room. My shame was never strong enough to deter me, though. Even as I wallowed in it, letting it sink its persistent claws into my exhausted limbs, I unzipped my portfolio and removed last night's stencil—of Ronald Reagan wearing Mickey Mouse ears—and slid it behind my dresser to keep it safe and out of sight.

I knew I would be back out there. Not tonight. Not even tomorrow night. But within a week, guaranteed.

I upended my backpack so I could refill it with the books and supplies I would need for classes and studio time today. Sorting through the pile of aerosol paint cans, I stashed the ones that were still good in the bottom of my closet. The two I'd used up, I stuffed into a garbage bag so I could throw them out in the Dumpster at work.

Then I crumpled up Jenny's phone messages and chucked those in too.

I smelled the pizza before I saw her. My stomach lurched when I caught a whiff of the garlicky, cheesy goodness. I hadn't eaten since last night's graffiti run, which was partly a function of my insane Tuesday schedule and partly a function of my broke-assedness. I had a shift behind the deep fryer at work tonight, though, and I'd be able to eat my fill then.

That's what I'd told myself, anyway. But then this girl appeared in the studio with a pizza box, waltzing right in like she owned the place. I was pretty sure she wasn't an art student. The art girls tended to sport more extreme looks, most of them somewhere on the spectrum between flirting-with-Goth and Bride of Frankenstein. The pizza fairy, though, with her teal-and-lemon-yellow-striped sweater and a huge, floppy, sparkly teal bow in her shoulder-length brown hair, looked like she'd been barfed up by Rainbow Brite.

"I thought you might be hungry," my unnaturally perky visitor said.

I didn't say anything, just tried to figure out what the hell she was doing in my studio as I looked her up and down. She was wearing a pair of translucent teal plastic shoes. Who knew there was so much teal in the world?

"I'm Jenny. Jenny Fields."

I raised an eyebrow.

"The editor of the *Allenhurst Examiner*?" she added, like I was supposed to know what that was. "The college newspaper?"

"Congratulations." I turned back to my easel, hoping she would take the hint, but my stomach chose that moment to growl so loudly it made her laugh. I'd been penny-pinching even more than usual this semester, trying to skim a little off every financial aid check to save enough for a deposit on a place in Boston after graduation.

"I knew you were hungry! I've been waiting in the hall for you to come out for two hours. So I thought to myself, if he's been working all this time, he must be hungry." She popped open the pizza box, and I almost groaned as she plopped it down on the table that held my supplies.

"What are you painting?"

I tried to move my body to block the easel but, man, she was fast.

"A telephone?" She squinted at the watercolor I had under way. Curry assigned me an exercise every week, and this one was to choose a mundane object and render it in every medium: oil, watercolor, acrylic, charcoal, pastels, yada, yada, yada. The cord in this version was giving me trouble, and it looked terrible. "And here I thought if you were working in here so diligently for such long hours, you were probably painting your own *Guernica*."

I said nothing.

She sat down.

Well, hell. If I couldn't eject this ridiculous person, I was going to have a slice of her pizza. She'd ordered pepperoni, peppers, and onions, which, strangely, was my favorite. My stomach growled as I picked up a piece. "Unnhh." I couldn't help closing my eyes against the wickedly good taste of that first bite.

She cleared her throat.

"So what can I do for you, Rainbow Brite?"

"Jenny. My name is Jenny."

I nodded, folded my second slice of pizza in half, and shoved it in my mouth.

"I'm trying to save this building," she said, looking around the run-down studio. When I didn't say anything, just kept eating, she added, "You've probably seen the editorials in the paper?"

"Nope."

"Or maybe you heard about the sit-in we staged?"

I shook my head.

She opened her mouth, then shut it again, as if she'd thought better about what she'd been planning to say. Her forehead furrowed so deeply above her light brown eyes that she almost looked like a cartoon. Befuddlement was actually kind of cute on her. I would have laughed if my mouth hadn't been full.

"Well, anyway, I'm trying to get the administration to reverse its decision to tear down this building."

I *had* heard about that. It wasn't happening until the summer, and I'd be gone by then, assuming I passed the goddamn senior portfolio. "You want some?" I nodded at the pizza, realizing that since I'd finished half of it in about thirty seconds, I should probably offer her some.

"It's a gorgeous old building." She was clearly trying to engage me in conversation about the doomed structure.

"It's also poorly lit and falling apart, and the ventilation sucks," I said, partly to be contrary but partly because it was the truth. "You're lucky I'm not working in oils, or you'd be halfway to passing out."

"So you don't care that this Gothic Revival masterpiece, the second-oldest building on our campus, is going to be thrown away as if it was no more than a piece of garbage?"

I helped myself to another slice—damn, that was good pizza. "That is correct."

"So you won't help me?"

"Help you what?"

"Save the art building."

"That would be a no."

She stood then—finally—her glossy pink lips pursed. She was pissed. I tried not to laugh but wasn't quite successful. I couldn't help it. The juxtaposition between the righteous rage and the innocent, brightly hued girl who was its source was too funny.

But I didn't have time for funny. I didn't have time for anything. My eyes were on the prize: graduation and then a place in Boston, where I could start showing my stuff to gallery owners or find someone who would take me on as an artist's assistant. Or, hell, get a job flipping goddamned burgers while I looked for something better. But to do that, I needed to finish school. And to do *that*, I needed to maintain my focus. "Well, it's been great chatting with you, Rainbow Brite, but I need to—"

"Everyone says you're an artistic genius."

It was true. But that was because everyone was blind. I would admit I had some talent, and when I arrived at Allenhurst, I might have embraced the "genius" moniker. I'd been eighteen and full of confidence. The next four years had been about having that confidence undermined as I learned about everything I *didn't* know. Being self-taught before I got here meant I had zero technique and knew shit-all about the great artists of the past. Look at the painting that was currently kicking my ass, for example. I was being defeated by a goddamned phone cord. But Jenny didn't need to know about my self-doubts. It was easier to play the part. Hopefully doing so would help me get rid of her. "Genius is such a strong word," I drawled. "But I guess all my fans can't be wrong."

"You're being selfish," she shot back.

Huh?

"You're graduating this spring, so the loss of the art building won't affect you personally." She sounded like she was at the front of a lecture hall. "But you have a duty to the students who will come after you."

Okay, now *I* was getting annoyed. "I have a duty to *myself*. And right now that means getting this shit done." I gestured to my drawing. "So if that's selfish, sign me up." When she didn't say anything, I added, "That's your cue to leave."

I thought I saw a flash of hurt in her eyes, which was too bad, but I couldn't help it if she couldn't take a hint and had to be outright told to leave.

She huffed out a little breath and turned to go.

Guilty, and simultaneously irritated that I had let her get to me, I called after her. "Thanks for the pizza, Rainbow Brite."

CHAPTER TWO

JENNY

Matthew Townsend was an arrogant jerk. I hadn't been counting on that. I'd expected that we would chat like civilized people, agree to join forces, and then I'd be off on Art Building Rescue: Plan B. Instead, I'd been insulted by a jerky boy who couldn't even manage to keep his mouth shut as he inhaled the food I brought him. It had been all I could do not to gather that chin-length black hair that kept falling in his face, force it back with a brightly colored hair clip that would break up his uniform of uninterrupted black, and scream, "Wake up!" It was maddening how blind some people were to the world around them.

But okay. I was not a quitter. Quitters didn't get into Columbia J-school. I just needed a different tactic—namely, persistence. It was just like with Dad. When he was having an episode, you couldn't ask him once if he wanted to get out of bed and go outside. You had to ask him a hundred times. Wear him down. Till he was mad at you, even, but someone had to care about things like sunshine on his face, or movement for his limbs.

Just like someone had to care about the art building. And despite the fact that its salvation would be good for my résumé, I *did* actually care.

So, armed with Matthew's class schedule, dorm room number, and intel about his work shifts at the Allenhurst Tap Room—I hadn't aced Foundations of Investigative Reporting for nothing—I started inserting myself into his orbit and tried not to take it personally when he did things like, oh, stand at his full six foot two and snarl down at me like I was an annoying puppy.

"Rainbow Brite. Do I need to take out some kind of restraining order against you?" he said as I ran to catch up with him after his anthropology lecture let out.

I held up a sandwich. The first time I'd cornered him, after he came out of his dorm the morning after we met, I happened to be carrying a muffin I'd intended to eat later. When he'd eyed it with unmistakable interest, I'd handed it over and watched him wolf it down. That, together with the pizza he'd devoured, suggested that the way to this secure this guy's help might be through his stomach.

And, God, the way he looked at that sandwich, with so much intensity in his green eyes. With longing. If only I could get him to look at my...cause that way, too. I handed it over. "So you won't even ask Curry what he thinks about the art building?"

"We don't have that kind of relationship."

"You mean the kind where you talk?"

"That's exactly what I mean," he said, mouth full of turkey and cheddar. "He lectures me about my art being flat and passionless, and I nod and vow to do better. Rinse and repeat."

"But can't you even—"

"There's also the part where I don't give a fuck about the art building."

His excessive swearing still shocked me a bit, but I tried not to show it. "You don't care about the legacy your alma mater leaves to future generations?"

"You need a new tactic, Rainbow Brite. I told you, that shit doesn't work on me."

I had pretty much given up on correcting him when he called me Rainbow Brite. I didn't even bother pointing out that today I was wearing white jeans and a black-and-white-striped off-the-shoulder T-shirt, so I was about as far from a rainbow as it was possible to be. Usually, I wore this outfit with a red belt for a pop of color, but I purposely hadn't done so this morning in anticipation of seeing him.

"I'm actually employing two tactics simultaneously," I said, glancing pointedly at the nearly gone sandwich. "That's why I ply you with food. It's like you're starving to death or something."

He stopped chewing, and though I wouldn't have thought it possible, his ever-present scowl deepened. Wait. *Was* he starving? I had his schedule down to a science—I'd pretty much been trailing him for two days, minus a few breaks for classes and newspaper stuff, and now that I thought of it, I'd never seen him in a dining hall.

"I work at the Allenhurst Tap Room. I get to eat all the deep-fried garbage I can stomach."

Yeah. He worked at the infamous campus pub three days a week for six hours. (I was nothing if not thorough.) That wasn't enough for a tall guy like him. I was pretty sure I'd inadvertently hit on an uncomfortable truth. Should I apologize?

"Jennifer."

My stomach dropped. I would have known that low, entitled, almost-sneering voice anywhere. If only I could have recognized the entitled, sneering part when we were freshmen. And Royce Waldorf all up in my face was *not* what I needed right now.

"The name's Jenny, Royce." Why couldn't anyone call me by my name? And why was Royce falling into step beside us as we crossed the quad? Our mutual disdain was a well-established thing.

"Jenny's a nickname. You can't just be named Jenny."

"And yet she is."

Whoa. I don't know who was more surprised that Matthew was leaping to my defense, Royce or me. But sure enough, Matthew was staring at Mr. Big Man on Campus like he was nothing more than an inconvenient insect being momentarily tolerated. His expression, I noted with interest, was actually much more severe than the annoyed look he usually gave me.

"If you're looking for Nessa, she's probably in our room," I said, hoping to shake Royce. I was perfectly safe out here on the quad in the middle of the afternoon, but he still made me nervous.

"Why would I be looking for Nessa?"

"Um, because she's your girlfriend?"

"I wouldn't go that far." He sidled closer to me. So did Matthew from the other side.

"Well, Nessa would. So maybe you two need to have a little heart-to-heart." And break up. With Royce, the shit was going to hit the fan one way or another. It was just a matter of time. To my mind, the sooner the better. If only I could get Nessa to see it.

I sped up, hoping he'd take the hint.

He did not, just kept walking beside me—way too close.

"Was there something you wanted?" Matthew raised his eyebrows at Royce. When Royce didn't say anything, he added, "Because we're in the middle of a conversation here."

Royce stopped walking and held up his hands like he'd been shot. "Hey, man, don't have a cow. This frigid betty is *all* yours."

As we got a little farther away from him, Matthew muttered, "Preppy dickweed."

"Yeah, he's pretty much my nemesis. Has been since freshman orientation." I tried to make light of the situation, but even I could hear the shakiness in my voice. I hated that Royce could make me so vulnerable.

"What did you do to him to get his undies in such a bunch?"

I contemplated telling him. I wasn't above playing on his sympathies to get what I wanted. But I hadn't even been able to bring myself to tell Nessa, who actually deserved to know, so I settled for a vague version of the truth. "I didn't give him something he wanted. He's never gotten over it."

"And your roommate is dating him? That's harsh."

I almost told him that I feared the only reason Royce was hanging around with Nessa was to mess with me. What was it about this kid that made me want to tell him all this stuff I'd never told anyone? "Yeah, and I'm pretty sure she's going to come away with a broken heart."

"If she's lucky, that will be it. I don't trust that guy."

I struggled every day with where my responsibilities lay in this whole situation. Quiet, pretty, sweet Nessa was madly in love with Royce. She saw only the stylish, rich, popular athlete—the campus golden boy. Never mind that he was a second-year senior, aka too dumb and/or wasted to graduate in the normal amount of time. Though he did seem to treat her well enough when they were together. Maybe he had changed. But then I thought back to his hands, groping me. To his drunken laughter when I pushed him away. Did guys like that ever really change? But I didn't want to think about that now, much less talk about it. I was supposed to be working on Plan B.

"I don't trust him, either," I said. "Untrustworthy *and* entitled. A charming combination."

"You gotta watch out for people born with silver spoons in their mouths," he said. Then he glanced at me. "No offense."

"What makes you think I was born with a silver spoon in my mouth?" It was kind of true. It was a small silver spoon—my mom had been a really successful real estate agent before she died, and my dad did okay as an architect when he was able to work—but still. I worked hard, and I hated the implication that I was undeserving of my success.

"I can just tell." He held up the wrapping of the sandwich I'd gotten at an off-campus deli. "This was a fancy sandwich."

It occurred to me that this was the longest exchange we'd ever had, even if the topic was making me kind of uncomfortable. Maybe I could turn things around with him after all. I brightened, thinking about the art building and Columbia. "Matthew Townsend, are we having a real conversation?"

We'd arrived at his dorm. "Nope." He pulled the front door open and called over his shoulder, "Thanks for the sandwich, Rainbow Brite."

I waved. I was totally making progress.

MATTHEW

I was always in a bad mood after a session with Curry, and tonight, as I got my graffiti stuff together to head out, was no different. That the man was a genius, I understood. He had never agreed to take on a senior portfolio student before. It was a huge honor, blah, blah, blah. What my faculty advisor failed to inform me was that Curry was also an asshole. And while my usual MO when dealing with assholes tended toward "go fuck yourself," I needed this particular asshole get my senior portfolio accepted, and hence to graduate.

"What is it you want?" he'd asked, earlier, at his studio, after taking one look at my studies of the telephone, pronouncing them "horseshit," and lighting a cigarette. The man smoked like a chimney, and the studio attached to his house was tiny (which was weird, because he was so famous), so the place was always hazy with smoke.

"I want to be an artist." He didn't know what a big deal it was for me to say that out loud. People from my background didn't become artists. They were considered wildly successful if they got steady jobs dealing cards at the casino or working at the gas station. The fact that I had gone to college at all, much less to an elite liberal arts school in a posh Massachusetts town eight hundred miles from home, was almost unheard of. So what I should have done to fulfill the whole "poor boy made good" thing was to pursue an actual career, something lucrative. Like a doctor or a lawyer. But, hey, I figured I was already used to being poor, so art it was.

"What you have here"—with a flick of his wrist, he brushed my paintings and drawings off the table they'd been spread out on—"are some pictures. What you have shown me so far this year is that you are a person who makes pictures. You are not an artist."

I swallowed my frustration. "I don't know what you want from me."

"Yes, you do. Your entrance portfolio was better than this shit. *That* stuff was why I agreed to take you on. There was a spark in that work. Feeling."

He was talking about the works I had submitted to be accepted to Allenhurst as an art major. And they *weren't* better. They were amateurish and naïve, and, nearly four years later, I was embarrassed by them. I had learned so much in my classes, had my eyes opened to technique and to the canon. It was why I endured the preppy cult-fest that was Allenhurst College. Why I killed myself getting A's and logging twice the amount of studio time I needed to. Why I shut out everyone and everything that wasn't getting me closer to my goal. Because I was getting *better*. Not good enough, I feared, but better. But Curry hadn't even glanced at that phone cord that had given me so much trouble.

"The assignment was to depict a mundane object," I said, wondering why I was bothering to argue. Experience had taught me that arguing with my so-called mentor never yielded anything but aggravation. "I don't know how much feeling a telephone can generate." For some reason, my mind had flashed back to all those phone messages from Jenny on my door. Maybe I should have drawn those little pink slips of paper—they had irritated the hell out of me. That was a feeling, right?

Curry stood. "We're done."

I had taken two buses to get into the city to meet him and missed a much-needed shift at the pub. And he had spent five minutes with me—and less than thirty seconds of that looking at my work. As the weeks slipped by and June drew closer, I was worrying more and more about my fate. The senior portfolio was supposed to be a big work, or a collection of smaller works, that functioned as an emblem of what the about-to-graduate student had learned. Our mentors and faculty advisors would jointly review and grade our efforts. It was the first week of April, and Curry and I hadn't even started talking about the actual portfolio. He just kept making me do these bullshit exercises and then tearing them down.

But I had been too proud to push him on it. To stand in front of him and say, "But what about my grades? What about not flunking out of college?"

That was the kind of thing Rainbow Brite would do. She would push and push and push until she got what she wanted. I was not that sort of person. I was the sort of person who put off signing a lease on the crappy rooming house in Boston he'd arranged to move into in June out of fear he might not graduate.

I hoisted my backpack higher on my shoulders. I was the sort of person who went out under cover of night to deface public property.

As I pushed through the front door of my dorm, I forced my mind to stop dwelling on my session with Curry earlier that evening, on Curry riding me about the lack of emotion in my work.

No emotion, my ass. Curry wanted emotion? How about rage? Would that do?

I honestly didn't know whether my graffiti runs were about expressing anger at society in general—I acted like they were, making stencils that called out the hypocrisy of the Reagan administration—or at this picture-postcard town, with its rich hippies and entitled, coddled college kids. I didn't much care, to be honest. I just knew the anger was there. And when I was done, when I slunk back to my room with my hood up and my eyes burning from exhaustion, it wasn't, and I could go back to another few days of getting my shit done.

So. Time to work.

As I strode across the quad that linked the dorms to the campus proper, a feminine voice pierced my thoughts. "Get away from me, you pig."

Shit. I hugged the portfolio that contained the stencil —Mickey Mouse Reagan again because I hadn't had time to make anything new—close to my chest. The campus at two in the morning was usually pretty deserted. If I ran into anyone, it was generally packs of drunk kids who either said something sneering or didn't notice me at all.

With any luck, the couple having a fight up ahead wouldn't either, and I could just slip by.

"No, sweetheart. Not a pig. I'm the big bad wolf," slurred a second, masculine voice. Jesus. These rich fuckers and their melodramas. "You shouldn't be walking alone at night if you don't want to attract the big bad wolf."

The girl, whose face I couldn't make out because she was swathed in some kind of neon-pink hooded sweat-shirt, was trying to wrench her arms from the guy's grasp. Damn. Now I was going to have to find a pay phone and call campus security—this was evolving from a lovers' quarrel into something more sinister.

"Let me go, Royce, or so help me God, I will write about this in the paper. I will write about that other night, too. And I will name names. I will tell Nessa everything."

My knapsack clattered to the ground, and the *clang* of the metal paint cans hitting the ground, even through the nylon fabric of the bag, drew the pair's attention. Two sets of wide eyes turned toward me.

"Well, well, well, if it isn't Art Boy," Royce sneered. "You here to rescue your little cunt girlfriend?"

"No," I said calmly as I walked toward them. The scattered, abstract anger that always propelled me on my graffiti runs had crystallized into a deadly laser beam. "I'm here to do this."

I punched him so hard he toppled over.

Then I picked up my bag, pressed my hand against Rainbow Brite's lower back to give her a little push, and said, "Run."

JENNY

We didn't stop running until we were in the lobby of my dorm. The whole way, I kept thinking, *I'm going to tell him about Royce.* I had no idea why. It didn't make any sense. I had never told anyone. Not my RA, not my dad, not Nessa. So why was I going to tell this sullen kid who didn't even like me?

"Come up to my room," I said, still panting.

"What about your roommate?"

"She's gone home for the weekend, which I suppose is why her gorilla of a boyfriend is on the loose." He was holding his right hand gingerly with his left. The crack of bone on bone as his fist connected with Royce's jaw had been sickeningly loud. "But first let's get some ice for that."

I took off toward the dining hall, and to my surprise, he followed without protest. "Won't the cafeteria be closed?"

I shrugged, eyeballing the rickety gate secured with a padlock that looked like it had already given up the battle. I pulled a metal nail file out of my purse, and it only took a few seconds of jiggling for the lock to yield.

He whistled. "Damn. I never would have pegged you as a criminal. Do they teach breaking and entering at finishing school these days?"

"I didn't go to finishing school," I said, not even bothering to turn my head toward him so he could see my eyes rolling. "I'm going to be an investigative reporter."

"Of course you are."

"Well, if I'm not, then I'm really going to regret all these late nights in the newspaper office that require me to walk home across campus at two a.m. straight into the sights of dudes who are a hundred IQ points dumber than I am but who are also, maddeningly, about a hundred pounds heavier." I glanced over my shoulder at him. Was he...smiling? Not really, just the slightest hint of a smirk was tugging the corners of his mouth, maybe, and it disappeared the moment I registered it. But still. "Sometimes a crime in support of the greater good is justifiable," I said.

After filling a bowl with ice from the soda fountain, it occurred to me that since we were in a cafeteria, I should probably nab some food for my cranky, always-hungry knight. Besides, my late night at the newspaper office had made me peckish, too. "Come on," I said, leading the way into the kitchen hidden behind the buffet where we always lined up with our trays. "I'm starving."

I started opening cupboards, looking for something portable. "How about sandwiches?" I said, pulling out an extra-long loaf of Wonder Bread and moving to a wall of refrigerators. "We just need to find something to put in them—aha!" I held up a laughably large package of turkey cold cuts. "Oh, and industrial cheese, too!"

He had opened the next fridge but popped his head out from behind its door, doing the almost-smiling thing again. "Would madame desire some mustard?"

I burst out laughing at the enormous jug he held out. It must have been a gallon at least. "I'm more of a mayo girl," I said when I recovered myself. But then he silently produced an even bigger container of Hellmann's, and I totally cracked up again.

"Shhh," he said. "I admit, I didn't peg you as a criminal, but if you are one, I'm going to bet you're not a stupid one, so shut the hell up."

I clamped my mouth shut, hefted my groceries in one arm, balanced the bowl of ice in the other, and gestured with my head for him to follow me. I about lost it again when he did so carrying both supersize condiments with an unnaturally straight face. How he managed them with the backpack and oversize portfolio he also had, I don't know.

Somehow, we managed to make it from the crime scene to my second-floor room undetected. I dumped the food on my desk. "You want to just dunk your hand in this bowl?"

"Nah, I'm okay."

"You are not okay. Did you hear the sound when your fist connected with his face?" I started rummaging around in my half of the closet for something to use for a makeshift ice pack, settling on an old T-shirt that had seen better days. I spread it flat on my desk, dumped the ice on it, and tied up the opening at the bottom to fashion an ice pack. "You saved my ass out there, so humor me."

He rolled his eyes, but he took the homemade pack and wrapped it around his hand as he lowered himself onto my bed, sitting across it perpendicularly with his back against the wall it was shoved against. "Things did seem like they were about to get a little dicey out there."

There was my opening. I still wanted to tell him. And not because I hoped it would somehow make him want to help me with the art building. It was more just a strange compulsion to tell *someone* coming over me gradually but inexorably, like a tide. I had been keeping this secret for three and a half years, and I didn't want it anymore. And Matthew, as unsettling as he could be, made me feel safe. And that was…really, really weird. But if I examined the thought too much, I would lose my nerve, and more than anything, I needed to let my secret out.

"Yeah. Royce was one of the leaders of my freshman orientation group. I… God, this is so embarrassing now." I turned my back and started making sandwiches so I wouldn't have to look at him while I talked. "For about a millisecond there, I thought he was cool." I braced for the incredulous reaction I deserved, but it didn't come, so I kept going—with the story and the sandwich. "He kind of…fixated on me. Assaulted me with his charm, if you will. And I didn't know anyone at Allenhurst. I'm not from around here."

"Where are you from?"

The question surprised me. I think it might have been the first time Matthew had asked me something about myself. "Oregon. Just outside Portland." I turned and handed him a sandwich. "I was nervous," I said, returning to my story, trying to tell it without sinking myself back inside it. Usually when my mind went back to that night, I felt the emotions as strongly as ever. Now, though, I wanted to recount what happened in a detached way. I took a deep breath. "I was trying to make friends. I had been kind of...straitlaced in high school."

"You don't say."

He was grinning, so I perched on the bed next to him with my sandwich and used my free hand to punch him in the shoulder, but I made sure it was his uninjured side.

The teasing actually helped—a lot. It grounded me in the present, allowing me to stay outside the story as I told it. "Yeah, so Royce seemed...cool. Which, again, I realize makes me seem like an idiot."

"Nah. Royce seems like a master manipulator. If you didn't already know him, I'm sure he could seem appealing." He cocked his head. "Actually, no, he couldn't. But go on."

"Okay, well, the second night of orientation, there was a party in Hannover House. A bunch of guys with adjacent rooms opened them up for the party. They were all freshman pledges to one of the frats on campus, and lots of the older brothers were there, too, including Royce. I... drank too much."

"As I'm sure everyone did."

I shrugged, the casualness of the gesture belying the fact that I was actually clinging desperately to my vantage point as a detached storyteller. "I didn't have a lot of experience with drinking, and it kind of came on me all at once. I got up to leave, and Royce noticed I was unsteady on my feet. He asked if I wanted to come to one of the empty rooms and watch a movie."

"And you said yes."

"Of course I said yes," I didn't even bother trying to keep the self-disgust from my voice. "He was the coolest guy I'd ever met." I didn't know what was worse, actually, what happened that night, or the fact that I walked right into it.

"I'm sorry, Rainbow Brite." I whipped my eyes to his face. He'd spoken so quietly, so…sincerely, that it startled me. I don't know why a genuine, calm expression of sympathy was such a shock, but it was.

"It wasn't…what you're thinking. I wasn't adverse to a little, um, experience." I cleared my throat because my voice had become embarrassingly scratchy. "But not, you know, much beyond first base."

"I fucking hate that metaphor. But I'm guessing Royce had different ideas about things."

"Yes. And when I kept pushing him away, he tried to force me."

"But you said it wasn't—"

"Well, I was drunk, but not so drunk that I couldn't knee him in the groin."

"Ha!" He barked a triumphant laugh. "Atta girl."

"And that's it, pretty much." I sagged back against the wall, and though I hadn't maintained the detachment I'd been going for, strangely, the story didn't have the same power over me it'd had just minutes ago. In fact, now that it was out, I wasn't sure why this had been weighing on me so much. I was embarrassed even. Some dumb freshman got her boobs groped by a jerk. What else was new? "Sorry. I know it doesn't seem like a big deal, but—"

"I think it's a big deal."

My breath caught. I wanted to kiss him for saying that, for understanding. But that would be stupid. Plus, I was having trouble meeting his eyes. I didn't know how to be with this Matthew, the sympathetic, nonconfrontational one.

The phone rang. I didn't know whether to be relieved or annoyed, because I knew who it would be. No one else called me in the middle of the night.

Matthew curled his lip. Ah, there was the surly boy I'd come to know. "You have a *phone* in your room?"

I sighed and picked up said phone. "Hi, Dad."

MATTHEW

Who was this girl? The fucking queen of Portland? I thought of all those phone messages she had left me. For some reason, the idea that she had been making those calls from her room *on her own personal phone* riled me. Reminded me who she was. I had been starting to feel a little sorry for her, with all this Royce stuff. She was vulnerable under all her bluster. She was kind of funny, too. But she was also—like everyone else at this school—a rich kid with no idea how the world actually worked. It was good, though, because it reminded me who *I* was and why I was at this school. It snapped me back into my place. In two months, she'd be using her trust fund to cushion herself while she willed her way into an entry-level journalism job, and I'd be in a vermin-infested shithole room in Boston trying to hold out as long as possible before I caved and got a restaurant job.

"Listen to me. Dad. Listen."

She'd been talking this way to her father for a few minutes. It was hard to figure out what was going on. She would listen for a while, then start lecturing him, but then seem to get interrupted.

"The little white pill, Dad. Did you take your pill at breakfast?"

There was a long silence, during which she looked at the ceiling and—goddamn, was she *crying*? She wasn't making any noise, but a few tears were leaking from the sides of her eyes. I'd been eating my sandwich while she talked, planning to get up and go once I was done, but dammit, I didn't think I should leave her like this.

"This is a manic episode, Dad. It will pass."

More silence. She shook her head as she listened to him. "Dad. Listen to me. This is the last thing I'm going to say. You are going to hang up the phone now and go to bed. If you can't sleep, you're just going to lie there until the sun comes up. If you don't promise me, right now, on Mom's grave, that you are going to do what I'm telling you, I'm going to call an ambulance."

Some more silence, then a quiet "I love you, Dad."

She hung up the phone, but she didn't move at first, just sat there with her shoulders slumped, frozen. After a few beats of silence, I watched her straighten her spine like she was steeling herself for battle. I recognized the posture. It was pretty much how I went through the world every day. When she finally turned, she caught me looking at the phone. Well, really, I'd been looking at her hand. When she'd replaced the receiver in its cradle, she'd started drumming coral-tipped nails on the baby-blue plastic. "I know you think I have a phone in my room because I'm a rich, spoiled brat," she said. "But really, I have a phone in my room because my father has problems, and I'm afraid he'll kill himself if he can't call me when he's having a…spell."

Jesus. Her voice shook, and she wouldn't meet my eyes.

I had no idea what to say, so I just went with "Come finish your sandwich, Rainbow Brite." When she didn't move, I leaned forward, grabbed her hand, and tugged her back onto the bed with me. She came, and we sat side by side on her bed, our backs to the wall.

She picked up the sandwich she'd abandoned early in the story about Royce. "Thanks for rescuing me tonight."

"I have no doubt you would have castrated that fucker yourself had I not stumbled on the scene."

"Still. It was nice to have an ally."

I chuckled, noticing that she hadn't denied the castration part. She yawned. It was contagious, apparently, because I did too.

CHAPTER THREE

MATTHEW

When I woke with a start, I initially had no idea where I was. My first clue was the Scott Baio poster on the far wall of a room that looked like a squadron of My Little Ponies had pooped sparkly girl accessories on every flat surface. My second clue was the throbbing pain and huge bruise on my right hand.

My third clue was the fact that Rainbow Brite was going through my stuff, which, of course, jolted me fully awake. "What the hell?"

She turned, and she didn't even have the good grace to look guilty. "What part of 'investigative reporter' did you not understand?"

I vaulted off the bed, where I had apparently conked out, but it was too late. My stencil and cans of paint were all over the floor. She had seen everything.

"You're the anti-Reagan-graffiti person, aren't you? Your stuff is all over town!"

There was no point in denying it. I started repacking

my bag and gathering my shit, trying not to panic, trying to think what I could say or do to convince her to keep this to herself.

"I don't know why it didn't occur to me. Of *course* it's you. Oh my God! I love your work."

That surprised me. But then, I had learned in the past few hours that Rainbow Brite, with her breaking and entering and her dickweed-prepster balls-kicking, had a bit of a dark side underneath all that sparkle. "Yeah, well, I'm poor. My family's poor. I come from a poor town in a poor state. But that doesn't make us stupid. And trickle-down economics is an insult to our intelligence." I started putting the paint cans back into my backpack. "But so help me, Jenny, if you tell anyone about this, or…" Shit. She was the editor of the *newspaper*. I was fucked. What if she told on me? Would Curry drop me? Would the school call the cops?

"You just called me Jenny."

I hadn't even noticed.

"And don't worry. Your secret is safe with me."

"It is?" I thought her whole thing was truth over all, investigative reporting, blah, blah. "Isn't that, like, against the whole raison d'être of journalism?" Though I didn't know why I was arguing. I could be in deep, deep shit if she told anyone.

"Well, considering that not only did I tell you my humiliating Royce story last night, but you also found out my father is insane, what do you say we just call it even? Agree to keep each others' secrets?"

I remembered those tears. Her tone as she spoke to her father, as if he were the child and she the parent. Her hunched shoulders, carrying too much.

As incredible as it seemed, I could trust her. So I stuck out my hand for her to shake.

She smiled. A great big megawatt smile that lit up her whole face.

Then she leaned in and kissed me on the cheek, her lips impossibly soft against a day's worth of stubble.

She pulled away before I could fully take stock of the astonishing sensation of those lips. "I gotta go. Lock the door behind you when you leave." She grinned. "Hope your day is totally mint."

And then she was gone, the soft, baby-powder smell of her the only sign that she'd been there at all, leaving me blinking and looking up at a picture of Charles in Charge.

JENNY

Matthew shouldn't have been surprised when, at one in the morning, he emerged from his dorm room to find me sitting on the floor in the hall outside of it. I had thought he was smarter than that.

But no. He reared back, almost as if someone had hit him, and then he nearly tripped over me.

"Did you really think I was going to let this whole 'I'm the crusading social-justice graffiti-artist man-about-town' thing go with no further discussion?" I asked as I scrambled to my feet. "I mean, just because I promised not to tell anyone about it doesn't mean *I* don't want to talk about it."

He rolled his eyes, pulled up his hood, and took off down the corridor.

Whoa. I guess our little détente of yesterday evening

had only been a temporary thing. Still, I was undeterred. "How come your roommate doesn't get suspicious?"

"I'm in a single," he said, walking so fast I practically had to jog to keep pace with him.

"What about the other guys on the hall?"

"I'm kind of a loner."

"You don't say."

He was waiting for me at the door to the courtyard, holding it open for me. I shot him a grin as I sashayed through and pulled up my hood, trying to cover my surprise that not only was he *letting* me follow him, he was being kind of chivalrous about it.

Again with the eye rolling. But he said, "At least you didn't wear that horrible pink thing you can see from a mile away."

"Give me a little credit." I didn't bother telling him that I'd had to borrow the navy windbreaker I was wearing from Nessa, as it turned out I owned nothing suitable for skulking around alleys committing crimes. It was making me question whether I'd need to make some wardrobe changes before launching my investigative reporting career. I trotted after him as he turned from the block of dorms on to the campus proper. "So where are we going?"

"Rule number one: no talking."

"That rule is not going to work for me." I tried not to pant—he was still keeping up quite the pace.

He stopped then, but I had too much momentum going, so I couldn't keep from crashing into him. He growled. He actually *growled*. Then he turned and stooped so he could get right in my face. With his green eyes glowing in the streetlight and his head otherwise concealed by his hood, he looked like a supernatural creature. Or, you know, a petty criminal with really pretty eyes.

"Listen to me, Rainbow Brite. This is *my* show. If you're coming with me, you're playing by *my* rules. I've been doing this for three and a half years, and I haven't gotten caught yet. I'm not about to start now because you can't keep your goddamned mouth shut."

Well. Okay, that was fair, I guess. Honestly, I was surprised that he had accepted my presence at all. I'd been prepared to fight to get him to let me come. So I made a show of shutting my mouth and miming throwing away the key.

It was hard, though. Oh, it was so hard! First of all, just walking in total silence for ten minutes. Who does that? All I could do was sneak glances at him as I loped to keep up with his long, determined strides. There was something about him tonight. An intensity. Well, there was *always* an intensity about Matthew, but it was even more in evidence as he led the way through the gates that marked the southern edge of campus. Then, when we arrived at our destination, which was a construction site in the town proper, and he pulled out his stencil, I wanted to lob a thousand questions at him. *How do you decide where to paint? Do you even consider it painting? How many different stencils do you have? What does this one mean?*

But I kept my mouth shut as instructed. So I was shocked when he broke the silence with a whisper. "Speed is the most important thing once you start." He was struggling a bit to keep the stencil flush with the wall with one hand while shaking a can of paint with another.

"Let me hold this in place," I whispered, pressing my hands against the black paper cutout. I couldn't make out what it was from this close vantage point. He hesitated a moment, and I added, "Won't it be faster if I hold it?"

He must have agreed, because he moved like lightning,

spraying the openings in the paper with red paint, which would show up dramatically against the gray-painted plywood fence surrounding the site. It took only a minute, and then he stepped back and nodded for me to do the same.

"Oh!" I gasped. It was Reagan again, but he was holding a lightsaber. *"Star Wars!"* He had interpreted the president's sinister plan to arm the heavens as straight out of the movie *Star Wars*. It took my breath away how a single image could make such a powerful statement. I couldn't take my eyes off it. It was silly, but I felt like I helped the tiniest bit, since I'd held the stencil, and been, like, an accessory.

"Yeah, I'm working on a matching Gorbachev, but it's not done yet."

"It's…perfect." It was. It was a simple image that managed to, in a matter of seconds, make you think about a wider political issue in a whole new light. Me, I talked a lot. I wrote. I wrote many, many words. But this? This was something else entirely, something beyond language.

Then it hit me all at once, a new, astonishing thought replacing the Plan B I had been so doggedly pursing. Maybe I didn't need Matthew to get to Curry. Maybe I just needed Matthew.

"Someone's coming."

Oh, crap. Sure enough, I could hear voices at the far end of the block, where the construction site started. I reached down to try to shove the stencil back into the portfolio, but he stopped me, pulling me around so my back was to the fence. "I'm just trying to get this out of sight," I tried to explain. "So—"

And then he was kissing me.

Matthew Townsend was kissing me.

And, like his art, Matthew's kisses were jolting. A revelation. There was no lead-in. No windup. He just grabbed the sides of my head and crashed his mouth down on mine. I don't know if it was the shock or what, but my knees actually buckled a little. Because it felt like my lips —no, *his* lips—were directly connected to my clit, which was suddenly throbbing and achy. He responded by pressing me back against the fence, using one of his legs between my own to prop me up. When he tilted my head farther back, I let my mouth fall open, and his tongue brushed against mine. I couldn't help the moan that escaped. It was like I wasn't in charge of my own body. I might as well have been a figure he was painting, he was that in control—not in a scary way, just that what was happening felt inevitable. So I performed my role, which right now seemed to require me to twine my arms around his neck and shamelessly kiss him back. It was everything I could do not to rock myself against the thigh that was propping me up.

He made a noise that was something like a cross between and grunt and a groan and tore his lips from mine. He let his forehead rest against mine for a heartbeat before stepping away completely, leaving me feeling exposed. Cold.

"They're gone."

I blinked, confused. "Who's gone?"

"The people who walked past us just now."

I followed his gaze. I caught a glimpse of a couple at the end of the block just before they turned the corner. The woman wore heels and the man a suit.

Right. That had been a decoy kiss, not a real one. I cleared my throat. "Quick thinking." But oh my God, how mortifying. I felt like he *knew* that I was wet between my legs, and that he'd made me that way. "See?" I said, trying for a casual, teasing tone. "It's good I came with you."

He just shot me a questioning look I couldn't quite decipher.

"Because you can't make out with yourself," I added, realizing belatedly that explaining wasn't helping. "We should go, right?"

He stooped and rummaged around in his backpack. "Yeah. I just need to sign it." He produced a can of spray paint.

"Oh, you mean like tag it," I said. See? I was cool. I was in the know. I wasn't a lust-addled college student. Or at least I wasn't *only* a lust-addled college student.

"No, tagging's not really my thing. I respect it, but to me, graffiti isn't about marking my territory or anything."

"It's about saying something."

He ducked his head like he was embarrassed.

"It's using art to make a statement. And you should sign your art."

"Something like that." He made a dot in the bottom right of the picture using gold paint.

"That's it? Just a little gold dot?" I made a mental note to start looking for the same mark in his other pieces around town.

"Just a little gold dot." He shrugged. "I can't sign my actual name for obvious reasons. I had this random gold paint on me the first time I went out—this was in my hometown, years ago. I was probably eleven or twelve. It was from some Christmas project we were doing in school. I hadn't used it for the actual graffiti—because, really, who does graffiti in gold?"

"Disco graffiti artists," I said, laughing.

"Exactly. You're basically never going to see gold graffiti—or at least it's going to be rare—so I just impulsively added a gold dot as a way to distinguish the piece."

"Like a period at the end of a sentence." I understood the motivation. Punctuation was my department.

He laughed then. He actually laughed, and I was absurdly proud to have been the reason he did. "Yep. Like a gold period. And then it just became a thing." He rummaged around some more and produced another can. "Here. You sign too."

"Really? I didn't do anything."

"You helped."

I could feel my skin heat. An A on a test or term paper had never thrilled me like his praise. "Okay." I shook the can like I'd seen him do, aimed the nozzle, and deposited a dot next to his gold one. "Pink!" I couldn't help exclaiming in delight.

He just shrugged, put up his hood, which had fallen during our interlude, and turned, silently gesturing for me to follow.

MATTHEW

"Interesting."

The word punctured the heavy, smoke-filled silence in Curry's studio, a silence that had been stretching on as my critic circled the table on which I'd unrolled my latest crack at the "make a picture of something mundane in every medium" assignment. Curry hadn't told me to do it over. We hadn't spoken at all, in fact, since my last visit, which was pretty much unheard of. He usually called me midweek and issued mumbled instructions for what he wanted to see at our next session. The fact that he hadn't worried me.

Anyway, I was stubborn—and proud. Even though I told myself I just wanted to extract a senior portfolio from this "mentorship" so I could graduate, in truth, I couldn't stand Curry thinking poorly of my work. So, even though I technically had no assignment this week, I had taken it upon myself to perform a do-over.

Curry was nodding and sucking on his cigarette as he made another circle, stopping in front of my rendering of the shirt in acrylics.

I was half bracing for him to dismiss me in disgust like he had last week, but my heart sped up a little when he said, again, "Interesting." Curry had never said that to me about anything, and tonight he'd said it twice.

"Where did you get this?" He tapped the image. "It clearly isn't yours."

It was a Duran Duran T-shirt, white, with the woman from the *Rio* album cover on it, and the sleeves were ripped off in the way that only girls seemed to be into. So, yeah, you didn't have to be a genius to see that it wasn't mine. "It belongs to a girl I know."

He took a step back and lowered himself into the frayed armchair he sometimes sat in while presiding over my fate. "And how did it come into your possession?"

Jesus. What did it matter? It was a mundane object.

Well, technically, it wasn't. In the context of Jenny's colorful, over-the-top room, it was a mundane object, which is probably why she'd chosen it to use for the ice pack. But in my room, lying crumpled on my desk with the woman's red lips and purple earrings visible, it was whatever was the opposite of mundane. Abnormal? Extraordinary?

Curry was still waiting for an answer. How had the shirt come into my possession? I wasn't about to tell him I'd stolen it. That I'd dumped the half-melted ice back into its bowl and pocketed the shirt before I left her room. That I had no idea why. "She gave it to me to use as an ice pack—she'd filled it with ice."

"And why did you need an ice pack?"

"I hurt my hand." I could see the next question forming and preemptively answered it. "I hit someone. Hard."

His eyebrows lifted.

"Someone who deserved it," I added quickly. *Please let that put an end to the interrogation.*

He stubbed out his cigarette and, uncharacteristically, didn't light another. "What were you feeling when you painted this shirt? What does looking at it now make you think?"

It makes me remember kissing her.

But I couldn't say that. *Wouldn't* say that.

"You don't have to answer out loud," he said, drumming his fingers on the arm of the chair. "But go there."

Even as I tried to resist his instructions, my mind obeyed. It wasn't hard—that was where my thoughts had been pretty much constantly since that night. It was like there was a groove worn in my psyche that my mind slipped into by default. The fear of being caught. The full-body shock of that kiss, the purpose of which was supposed to have been to distract the passersby. A couple of kids making out was better than a couple of kids defacing public property, right?

But then...her lips, soft and pliant. Opening for me as she went limp and heavy.

The tiniest of rolls she made with her hips against my

thigh—I don't even think she was doing it consciously. The jolting idea that *Jenny Fields* wanted *me*. Maybe not for real. But in that moment there, against a construction fence at two in the morning, she had. It was astonishing.

Curry's chuckle punctured my little trip down memory lane. Jesus, I was close to popping a woody, too. Time to get my head in the game.

"Now we're getting somewhere, Townsend."

We were? If I'd known that all I needed to do to impress Curry was paint a stupid Duran Duran T-shirt, I'd have done it months ago. Did I dare bring up the portfolio? I cleared my throat. "I was wondering what you thought about my senior portfolio?" I ventured, hating the way I sounded all deferential.

"I don't think about it," he answered, lighting a cigarette, standing, and brushing off his pants—all actions I recognized as presaging my dismissal. "Not yet. But bring me more of this"—he waved his hands vaguely toward the shirt images—"next week."

"You want more still lifes?"

Curry reached for his pack of cigarettes. "No, I want more emotion."

I nodded, still not sure what that even meant.

"And I want it in the form of a portrait."

CHAPTER FOUR

JENNY

"It's for you." Nessa tossed the phone's receiver at me. We'd been lying in our beds Saturday morning talking before getting up. Well, she'd been talking. I was trying to screw up my courage to tell her about Royce. Telling the story out loud to Matthew, seeing him react so strongly, made me feel extra guilty about keeping something so important from her. Didn't she deserve to know what kind of guy she was dating?

"Hello?" I said as Nessa started gathering her shower stuff.

"Hey. Rainbow Brite."

I sat straight up. That voice I used to think of as sullen was low and scratchy, as if he'd just woken up. And it was frustratingly powerful. How could someone's voice over the phone make my nipples tingle and tighten? It didn't seem fair.

"I haven't seen you around this week."

It was true. I had abandoned my campaign of

following him. Our mismatched reactions to that kiss were too mortifying. The fact that I'd thought it genuine made shame flood my gut anew. I hadn't made any headway on getting him to help with the art building, so what was the point of trailing around after him like a besotted puppy? I had to have *some* pride, even at the expense of the art building. "Yeah. I've been busy."

"Too busy to sit for a portrait?"

"What?" I must have said the word with the same vehemence as the sentiment in my head, because Nessa, in her robe and poised to depart for the bathroom, turned and raised her eyebrows at me. I waved her off and waited until she'd left before turning back to my call. "I'm sorry, say that again?"

"Curry is making me do a portrait, and I need a model."

"What?" Sheesh, I was going to have to think of something else to say.

"Model," he said, speaking slowly and enunciating each syllable. "I want to draw you."

"But why?"

He didn't answer, and I listened for a moment to the soft static on the line. As the silence stretched out, I realized what he wasn't saying. He didn't have anyone else to ask.

"Okay," I said, partly against my better judgment. "When?"

When we'd hung up, I opened my closet. What did a girl wear to be drawn? My eyes caught on a flash of blue. Did I dare?

I dared.

After I was dressed, I threw my wallet and keys into my favorite purple LeSportsac and opened the small top drawer where I kept my toiletries. There was something I'd been thinking about, even before I met Matthew. Something I wanted dealt with before graduation. And now that I *had* met Matthew, now that I knew about the sensations he was capable of inspiring, he seemed like he might be just the man for the job. Did I dare?

I dared.

MATTHEW

An hour later, she walked in the door of the same studio she'd invaded with her pizza two weeks ago, and my breath caught a little bit. It was probably because I wasn't used to things being easy. Nothing had ever been easy—*ever*. So the idea that I could just call this girl I hardly knew, and say, 'Hey, can I draw you?' And then she would just show up? I…didn't know what to do with that.

"I'm overdressed."

I had heard the phrase "struck dumb" before, but it always seemed…dumb. But damn, there was Jenny in an electric-blue off-the-shoulder dress with one of those bubble-type skirts that folded over itself instead of hanging straight like a normal dress. She *was* overdressed, and she was completely not my type, but she was also utterly stunning.

"This was my prom dress." She rolled her eyes in a self-deprecating way that almost made me wince. An investigative journalist in a dress like that shouldn't be mocking herself. "Well, that's not really true. It was *supposed* to be my prom dress, but I didn't actually go to prom."

"There's no such thing as overdressed in a portrait," I said, wanting to put her at ease, and for her to keep talking. I told myself that if she kept talking, she would relax, but to be honest—and to my dismay—I also wanted to hear the story. "Whatever you want to wear is great." I settled her on a chair a yard or so away from the easel where I'd set up to do her in pastels—I wouldn't have to wait for them to dry, and I could take the portrait to Curry and be done.

So I picked up a peacock-blue pastel, aiming for the insane color of that dress. "Why didn't you go to prom?" She probably wouldn't answer, but hey, I had to try.

She blew out a breath that fanned out her already-poufy bangs. "It's not some horrible story of being jilted or anything. I was supposed to go with a friend of mine—just as friends."

There was something in the way she said it that made me suspect she'd hoped for more. But I couldn't ask about that.

She made an exaggerated shrugging motion, and the self-deprecation was back in full force. "But then the girl he *really* liked broke up with her boyfriend, so of course I had to step aside so he could ask her."

Idiot. I bit my tongue to prevent myself from saying the word aloud.

"I should have just returned the dress." She smoothed her hands down the satiny bodice. It was a nervous gesture, but, Jesus, I had to shift to make sure I was hidden behind the easel so she couldn't see the effect she was having on me. "But I really loved it. Wearing it made me feel totally bitchin'. So I told myself I'd have an occasion to wear it someday, and I packed it up and brought it to college, which is pretty much the stupidest thing ever."

"Nah," I said. "College seems like it's going to be a really big deal. And then you get here."

She giggled. "Right? So it's been in my closet for almost four years now."

"No sorority formals for you?" I said. I'd meant to tease, but I found myself thinking of Royce and his type, and the lightness left me.

"Are you kidding me? Totally not my scene." When I didn't say anything, she added, "I know you think I'm some kind of rich-girl lightweight, but—"

"I don't think that." The interruption was kind of rude, but I couldn't let her go on without correcting the record. Though I was probably protesting too much. I *had* thought that, but obviously I'd been wrong.

She had narrowed her eyes at me the moment I interrupted her, and she silently regarded me through them, until all of a sudden, she grinned. "So when you asked me to sit for you, I thought, what the hell? I love this dress, and I'm obviously never going to have an occasion to wear it unless I make one."

She rolled her eyes again, but this time it wasn't in a mocking way, it was just...joy. Mischievousness. I drew faster, trying to capture the contradictions that constituted Jenny. She was embarrassed but shameless. Timid but brave. It should have been impossible. *She* should have been impossible.

After a few minutes of companionable silence, she said, "Do I have to be quiet to, like, respect your artistic process or something?"

I was tempted to say yes because I could tell just from looking at her that being quiet was torturing her, and I could extrapolate that if I let her speak, she would somehow have accumulated an hour's worth of things to say in the five minutes of silence that had elapsed. But I went for the truth. I owed her that, didn't I, for spending a gorgeous Saturday morning inside posing for me? "Nah. I can pretty much paint or draw through anything. Growing up, my house was very…" I trailed off, trying to think how to put it, how to explain that I used to hide in my room while my parents shrieked and threw things at each other. "Loud," I finally said. "Once I painted through an auction."

"Like, with an auctioneer and everything? Going once, going twice?"

I nodded. "It wasn't like on TV, though. It was a lot more orderly than you'd expect."

"Did you buy anything?"

I shook my head. "Nope. It was our stuff that was being auctioned—our house had been foreclosed." I didn't look at her as I said that, just fiddled with the pastels to try to get her skin tone right. I wanted to tell her something true, but I didn't want to see the pity I knew would be in her eyes. "So I just set up an easel in the yard and tried to paint the house. I don't know why. I never had any partic-ular attachment to it."

"Kind of like you don't have any attachment to the art building."

That *did* make me look up. I didn't see any pity. She was just sitting there with her head cocked, teasing me.

I shrugged. "Buildings, houses—they're just bricks and mortar. Why get all fussed about them? They're all ulti-mately going to be dust anyway."

"Well, so are people, if you want to get technical about it."

I shrugged again, letting her fill in the blanks. Even I could see that outright saying I didn't care about people any more than I cared about buildings just made me sound like a jerk. "Why do you care so much?"

"I guess I just want to leave my mark on this school." She scowled. "Well, that's not totally true. I mean, it is true, but also, I'm planning to—"

"Not the art building," I interrupted. "Why do you care so much about *everything*?"

She inhaled. Not quite a gasp, but a sharp intake of breath I thought might signal that I'd hit on a truth she wasn't completely comfortable with.

"Isn't it better to care too much than not to care at all?" Her voice was low, almost a whisper.

"Probably." She was certainly a better person than I was—no argument there. "But that doesn't answer my question."

To my utter shock, her eyes filled with tears. I wasn't quite sure what was happening, why what I'd thought was an innocent question had spawned tears. "Oh, hey, don't cry, Rainbow Brite. I'm a jerk. Just ignore me."

She did what I asked, looking down at her hands and fiddling with her nails. Her coral nail polish from the other night was chipped and she started to peel it off one of her fingers. It made me realize that I didn't actually *want* her to ignore me, God help me. "I think it's cool that you care about things—and people. "

She was still playing with her nails, and she remained silent for a long time. When she finally spoke, she'd raised her voice from its previous whisper, and it startled me a little. So did what she said: "I can't fix my father, so I try to fix everything else." She still wasn't looking at me, but I could see a single tear begin its journey down her cheek.

I kept drawing.

"I never thought about it like that until just now, but I'm pretty sure that's the truth." She moved from her nails to her skirt, fiddling with the ruffle. "I'm terrified my father is actually going to kill himself one day, and I'll be alone. So I guess I have to care about everything else so that when that happens, I'll have...something."

I had heard her reference her mother's grave over the phone the other night. "No siblings?"

She shook her head, wiping her eyes with her fingers.

"Has your father always...had problems?"

She cleared her throat. "I think so. When my mom was alive, I didn't pay too much attention, to be honest. He definitely had down periods where he slept a lot, and my mom always told me not to bother him. But then my mom got sick—breast cancer—and I sort of..."

"Took over."

I could see it. Functionally speaking, she was her dad's parent. Just like she went around trying to look after everyone and everything at Allenhurst.

"The worst part is that if anything does happen to him, it will be my fault."

Geez. Who knew that sunny Rainbow Brite had been carrying such a burden around all this time? "How do you figure that?"

"I knew my dad was sick. So why did I decide to come to a school that was three thousand miles away? What kind of sense does that make?"

"You deserve to have a life, Jenny. Your own life. You can't be responsible for him. Maybe some subconscious part of you understood that and ran away." It wasn't that different from what I'd done, really, though my escape to Allenhurst College had been fully premeditated. It was what I'd been working toward every minute of every day from the time I was old enough to understand that college could be my ticket out of my town. My ticket out of my family. My ticket to becoming an artist, something I wanted so badly I could scarcely allow myself to think about it.

She smiled through her tears. "It still sounds so weird when you call me Jenny."

JENNY

Matthew worked on the drawing for a good three hours. It was a strange feeling to have someone looking at me so intensely. And of course it wasn't just that he was looking at my body, but that he'd somehow, with a simple series of questions, unearthed an elemental truth about me that I had never confronted before—that I was always running around trying to fix things because I couldn't fix my dad. That much scrutiny was strange, but I'd agreed to be his model, so all I could do was sit and try not to fidget under his appraisal.

But he put me at ease, which was kind of incredible when you considered that a couple weeks ago, he was basically a snarling mute. After the heaviness of our initial conversation, we talked easily. He told me a little about the town he was from, but I noticed he avoided any details relating to his parents—though I had learned that he had a much older sister who left home when she was sixteen and he was eight. But mostly we just talked about mundane things. I had a million questions about his family, his plans after graduation, and all that, but it didn't seem appropriate to ask them while he was working.

I had just started to wonder how I could delicately ask him if we could pause for a bathroom break when he stood and stretched.

"A break?" I asked, hopping up from my stool.

"Nope. All done."

"Oh!" I had no idea how long these things were supposed to take. "Can I see?" I started toward him, but he froze and his eyes darted around like he was a caged animal. "It's okay," I said, taking a step back. "You don't have to show me." But damn, I wished he would.

"No. It's okay. Come take a look." He pressed his lips together and beckoned me over. "It's just that it's always kind of weird to show your stuff to someone, and I've never actually done a portrait like this before."

"You've never done a portrait?" It was hard to believe.

"Well, sure, we've had models in class and stuff. But this is the first time I've drawn someone I actually…"

"Know?" I supplied.

"Like," he corrected, just as I stepped around to the front of the easel and caught my first glimpse.

My jaw dropped. It literally dropped.

He had drawn me not once, but twice. In each likeness, I was depicted from the waist up. On the left, I was crying a little—my eyes were all watery, and there was one tear on my cheek. I was staring into space wistfully, like I was thinking about something far away. Someone, rather, because I recognized the moment, even though I had experienced it from the inside and had not been able to observe myself in it as he had. It had been when he'd plucked out the truth about my fears about my father and my guilt over leaving him.

The second image, even though it was me, in the same dress, was the polar opposite of the first. I was looking right at the "camera" and cracking up. My huge grin exposed my teeth, and my eyes looked…happy. It seemed an anemic word to describe what I was seeing, but it was the best I could come up with. I tried to think when this moment had been, but unlike with the other image, I couldn't pinpoint this one. I realized that there had been several times something he'd said had made me laugh.

And…whoa. Hang on a second.

Matthew *liked* me?

"You hungry?" he asked as he stood at a sink at the far end of the room, washing his hands. I had to struggle to make sense of what he was saying, because my brain was still busy exploding. "Because I'm starving. What do you say we hit the A-Hole?" he said, using the Allenhurst Tap Room's more common nickname. "I can use my vast insider knowledge to steer you toward the least awful items on the menu."

"I should swing by my room and change first," I said, amazed that my voice came out sounding calm.

"Nah." He wiped his hands on a towel and looked me up and down. It was hard not to squirm. "You look great."

Ten minutes later we were ensconced at a table at the infamously grungy Allenhurst Tap Room, sipping pints of beer and eating mozzarella sticks. I had gotten some weird looks from the other patrons, what with my formal dress, but I'd taken my cue from Matthew, who seemed totally oblivious, and acted like everything was normal. "These are shockingly good," I said, laughing as a gooey mozzarella string extended from my mouth to the uneaten half of the stick I'd bitten into.

"Yeah, it's hard to mess up fried cheese," he said.

It being a Saturday afternoon toward the end of the term, the pub was crowded, so we had to lean close to make ourselves heard. He smelled like turpentine, which wasn't a surprise given that he was an artist. But the fact that I found it so irresistible kind of was.

"You do what you can back there," he said, nodding at the kitchen. "But given the quality of the ingredients, that's only so much. But cheese, even cheap cheese, is pretty reliable."

"You're quite the connoisseur," I said. The Hefeweizen he'd steered me toward, suggesting its lightness as a good foil for the rich cheese, was a perfect match for the mozzarella. "Have you worked here your whole time at Allenhurst?"

"Yup. And I am not going to miss it at all."

"What are you going to do after you graduate?" I almost didn't ask the question I'd been wondering about for so long. Things had become so easy between us, and it seemed like the type of question that might scare him off.

"What are *you* going to do?" he countered.

"Move to New York and get a job in journalism," I said. "Then after a year or two, I'm going to apply to Columbia for a master's in journalism." It had always been the plan. It was the one thing in life I could count on.

When he didn't say anything in response, I decided to push him further. (I'm a masochist, apparently.) "You ever think about New York? Isn't that the center of the art world?"

He was shredding a napkin. "Yeah. But I'm not sure you get to just *be* an artist."

"You already are one."

He looked up, surprise written across his face.

"You are," I protested. "That might be quite apart from your ability to make money from it, but I have no doubt that you are an artist of the finest ilk." It was the truth, and there was something about Matthew that kept making me want to tell him the truth.

"It's the money part that's the problem. If I'm just going to end up flipping burgers, why do it in New York, where everything is so expensive? I'm going to Boston. It's cheaper, and there will be no moving expenses—just me and my shit on the bus."

"Can't you do something related to art to make money? Like work at a museum, or—oh! Oh!" I had the perfect idea. I didn't know why I'd never thought of it before. "What about editorial cartooning?" He started to protest, so I just plowed on. "Seriously. Your graffiti is all about politics."

"Shh," he cautioned sharply, looking around. I felt bad —I'd been getting excited, and my voice had risen. "That's not art, though."

"Are you kidding me?" I wasn't much of an art person, but I searched my mind for an example of a politically minded artist. "Diego Rivera!" I cried triumphantly. "Are you telling me his stuff wasn't art?"

Matthew rolled his eyes. "You did not just compare me to Diego Rivera."

"All I'm saying is, you clearly have something to say. So why not editorial cartooning as a way to make money?"

"So I should just knock on the door of the *New York Times* and tell them I'm ready to go?"

There was a hint of his old snarling tone. I didn't like it. So I shot him a withering glance as I said, "No. I would think the first step would be to build a portfolio." When he didn't answer, I softened a bit and added, "It's too bad you don't have any ins with newspaper editors."

MATTHEW

Apparently I'd drunk the rainbow-flavored Kool-Aid, because half an hour later, watching Jenny trot back to the table from a trip to the restroom, I was preparing to capitulate to her demand that I submit a cartoon for next week's *Allenhurst Examiner*. I'd resisted as long as I could, but, as she had so vehemently pointed out, I owed her for sitting for that portrait. As she walked, bouncing along in her bright white Keds, the skirt of her electric-blue formal puffing up a little, I could feel the last shred of my willpower evaporating. I was pretty sure Curry was going to love my portraits of her. And though I would never admit it out loud, she kind of had a point about cartooning. It had never occurred to me as a possible job path, but what could it hurt to have a bit of practical art experience on my résumé? Even if I had to get some shit job to pay the bills, wasn't it a good idea to actively be adding to my portfolio at the same time?

Just as she arrived back at our table, a girl I didn't recognize did too.

"Nessa!" said Jenny, smiling. Ah, so this was the roommate. Warily, I looked around, only half paying attention to Jenny's introduction. If the roommate was here, it was possible that Royce wasn't far behind.

I'd been looking out into the bar proper, but he approached from the hallway behind us, where the restrooms were. And he wasn't alone. There were two other preppy types with him, complete with letter jackets and frosted blond hair.

"Art Boy."

I shot him a look. It wasn't like he was going to do anything in public, but I knew his type. I had punched him. Jenny had refused him. He would never let these slights go. Plus he was slurring a bit.

"Cat got your tongue, fag?"

"Don't use that language around me, Royce," Jenny said with a coolness I suspected was manufactured.

"What? 'Fag'? Would you prefer 'cocksucker'?"

The Neanderthals laughed, and Jenny's roommate gasped. "Royce!" she whisper-admonished, taking his arm.

He shrugged her off like she was an insect and let his gaze settle on Jenny. Silently, he took in the dress, which was, of course, wildly out of place in the casual pub, where acid-washed denim ruled the day. I wasn't looking to start anything, but I knew without a doubt that if he insulted the dress that Jenny so loved, I was going to punch him again. And I wouldn't stop at one this time.

"I'm just calling it like I see it," Royce said to Jenny's roommate. "If you couldn't tell from his pansy-assed long hair and artistic ways, we know it's true because this frigid chick"—he turned back to Jenny, leering—"wouldn't let a real man anywhere near her. Ergo, Art Boy is a fag."

"Ergo," I drawled. "Wow. Big word for you, Royce." This couldn't possibly end well. I didn't know how to defuse the situation, but I wasn't about to cower before Royce fucking Waldorf. "Bigots don't usually come equipped with such impressive vocabularies."

He took a step closer, a vein on his temple bulging.

"Is there a problem here?"

Never had I been more grateful to hear that voice. It was the pub's night manager, Brian. Though Brian was usually riding me about bussing tables faster or not letting the kegs sit empty, he was basically a stand-up guy.

"I hope not," I said. "My friend and I are just trying to enjoy a drink."

Brian turned to Royce, eyebrows raised. "Can I help you find a table?"

The intervention worked. After a few beats of tension-laden silence, Royce snarled and stalked away. Jenny's roommate, the last to follow, stood staring at Jenny for a few seconds. She looked like she wanted to say something, but Jenny wasn't cutting her any slack. She just stared back, her eyes hard. Good for her. If this Nessa chick was going to choose Royce over Jenny, the correct response, if you asked me, was *good riddance*.

But of course Jenny didn't ask me; she just looked up at me once her friend was gone, those huge brown eyes filling with moisture. "How could she just stand there and listen to him talk to me like that? To both of us?"

I shook my head, not sure what to say. For someone with a dead mom and a messed-up dad, she was amazingly innocent in some ways. How did you tell someone like Jenny that it's better to expect the world to fuck you over because that way you're not disappointed when it does?

"How am I going to face her back at the room tonight?" Her voice was small, and I didn't like it. I didn't like it at all. Small didn't suit her.

"Will she stay with Royce?" I asked. Not that I wanted to subject anyone—even the thoughtless, self-absorbed Nessa—to Royce. But for Jenny's sake, it would be better if her roommate just didn't come home tonight.

She shook her head. "I don't think so. When he's that drunk, she usually comes back to our room."

Well, then. There was only one correct course of action to take. I stood up. "Let's get out of here."

CHAPTER FIVE

MATTHEW

"I can't just hide out in your room indefinitely," Jenny said, even as she lowered herself to perch on the edge of my bed, which, since the desk chair was covered with a painting I'd draped there to dry last night, was the only place in the small room to sit. My room was a disaster, actually, strewn with clothes and art supplies. In her fancy dress, she looked like a princess in a hovel.

Normally, I would have agreed with her. I didn't like having people here. Hell, I didn't like people generally, which was why I avoided the other guys on the floor. And since I didn't have a dining package, I didn't have to deal with them in the cafeteria, either. People came with shit—emotions, demands, needs—that would only distract me from doing what needed to be done. But, somehow, more than I didn't want people in my room, I didn't want Jenny to risk another run-in with Royce or Nessa. Obviously, she was going to have to see her roommate at some point, but just…not yet. But I couldn't say that without sounding like an idiot. "You don't have to stay. Just give me five minutes. I want to show you something." I cleared the desk chair, sat down, and rummaged around in the desk for a fresh sheet of paper and a fountain pen. "But I was thinking…" I twisted to look at her over my shoulder. "If you stay until it gets really late, she might be asleep when you get back to your room." I shrugged. "Whatever you want. But you're welcome to stay as long as you like."

She shot me a grin. "Thanks." Then she used each big toe to slip off the opposite foot's shoe and swung her legs up so she was half sitting, half lying back against my pillows.

I should have stopped staring at that point. She clearly wasn't going anywhere, at least not immediately. It's just that the sight was so incongruous. Rainbow Brite, all sandy brown and electric blue, glossy and tough, innocent and bold, sprawled out on my bed as if she belonged there. And her dress had hiked up a bit as she'd laid back, exposing a pair of smooth pale thighs.

I had managed to sublimate pretty much every biological urge I'd had since coming to college. I ate just enough to keep me going, trying to spend as little money as possible on what I forced myself to regard as mere fuel. I drank water. It was free, and there was no danger of too much water impairing your judgment.

I hadn't had sex since high school. The girls I'd slept with back then had been enjoyable diversions, and they'd come on to me. It sounds awful to state it so clinically, but they were there for the taking, so I took. That didn't happen at Allenhurst. Besides, I hadn't really even looked up long enough in my time here to make lasting eye contact with anyone. I had no time for relationships—this phase of life was about getting good grades, learning actual technique in my art, and working enough to survive. It was about getting what I needed to set me up for the next phase, when my real life would begin. So if I was horny, I'd close my eyes and beat off to an imaginary girl.

And she never looked anything like the real one currently draped across my bed.

"What?"

The imaginary girl of my masturbatory fantasies also didn't talk.

"You're looking at me like something is wrong," she said.

I turned back to the desk and shifted in my seat, trying to ease the pressure that had built in my groin. Something was wrong, that was true. But that wasn't why we were here. I was used to self-denial, so better to just get on with it. I picked up the pen, and she seemed to accept that I wasn't going to say anything, because for the next few minutes the only sounds in the room were the scratch of my pen and her soft breathing.

When I was done, I turned my desk chair around to present her with the fruits of my labor.

"What's that?" she asked, sitting up and scooching to the edge of the bed to peer at the paper I held.

Here we went. Silently, I handed her the drawing.

There was no noise in the room while she absorbed it. I was struck suddenly with the urge to minimize my efforts. "You sat for the portraits," I said, feeling my face grow warm. "So I figured the least I could do was give you a cartoon in return." It was about the goddamned art building. I'd drawn a little picture of a crowd protesting outside it, except the crowd was made up of famous artists that regular people were likely to recognize: da Vinci, Andy Warhol, and so on. It wasn't the most imaginative thing, but it was the best I could do on the spur of the moment.

She looked up, and...shit. To say the smile that blossomed lit up her face would be an understatement. It might as well have been powered by the same neon that made her dress blaze that fierce blue. But at the same time, her eyes had grown suspiciously dewy. She was full of contradictions, this one.

I expected a torrent of words. I knew her ways now, and after she got over her shock that her campaign had finally succeeded, she would start talking and stop maybe sometime tomorrow or the next day.

I did not expect her to kiss me.

My single room was so small that there were only a couple feet between the bed and the desk. Since she'd moved to the edge of the bed, all she had to do was lean forward. She pressed her lips to my cheek and murmured, just before they hit, "This is wonderful."

I froze. I hadn't shaved in a couple days, so I had more than a five-o'clock shadow going. Her lips were too soft for me. *She* was too soft for me.

But I couldn't move. I couldn't push her away. I just sat there, letting her put her mouth against me like a brand.

It was a chaste kiss, on the surface of things. It was just her lips against my cheek, and her hands rested in her lap, for fuck's sake. But, just like the other night, at the construction site, it was like she was filling me with lava. It ran down my throat, swirled around my chest, and then settled in my dick, where it burned hot and fierce.

She pulled away, but only slightly. "Thank you for this," she whispered. See? This was what nice girls did.

They said thank you. They kissed you on your rough cheek.

Though she'd moved back enough to speak, she hadn't returned to sitting upright on the bed. She stayed leaning forward, listing toward me, bracing her hands on her thighs.

I let my gaze slide over a bare neck that would make Degas weep. Across pale, unblemished shoulders. The bodice of her dress went straight across, a horizontal ruffle making a dramatic line between white skin and brilliant blue dress. Earlier, it hadn't been showing much in the way of cleavage, but now that she was leaning forward, a gap had appeared between the ruffle and her breasts.

I couldn't stop looking at that gap. Why didn't she just move back? She had her cartoon. She'd deposited her perfunctory kiss. We were done here.

Weren't we?

"I don't want to graduate a virgin," she whispered.

A jolt shot through my body. I could feel each rib painfully expanding as I sucked in a breath and brought my eyes up to look into hers. In contrast to the tentative tone of her last sentence, her eyes were fierce, glittering, determined. Those were the eyes of the investigative journalist she would become.

"I have a sponge in my bag," she added, her voice catching a little.

"Oh, Rainbow Brite," I said, though it came out sounding more like a groan. I let my head fall to my chest. I couldn't look at her anymore. The room should have been silent then, but I swear, the blood in my ears was like thunder.

She might have spoken and I hadn't heard her, because the next thing that happened was she moved her hands from her thighs to mine. She just laid them there, but it was nearly enough to make me black out.

I flinched. I was startled, turned on, wary…everything. Everything all at once.

"I'm sorry," she said, snatching her hands away.

No. The protest probably started with my dick, to be honest, but it rose up through my chest and down through my legs simultaneously, spreading until it swirled throughout my whole body, propelling me toward her.

I wasn't going to be the reason Jenny Fields was sorry.

I was also done being a goddamned monk.

So I grabbed her and fell back onto the bed, hauling her on top of me. She shriek-laughed in delight, and it did something to me. The ribs that had twinged before were opening like doors now, but it wasn't smooth. It wasn't pretty. It felt like my chest was cracking open, jagged bits of bone piercing pathetic, inadequate lungs I couldn't get enough air into. So I did the only thing I could do, which was to kiss her. She melted into me immediately, straddling me with her legs and letting her whole weight settle on me as she sighed and opened her mouth.

JENNY

When I pushed open the door to Matthew's room, I sent a silent prayer to the sky. *Please don't let him have changed his mind.* (Also: *Please let me have inserted that sponge correctly.*) If I had been on the pill, this awkward interruption of the action wouldn't have been necessary. We could have gone right from rolling around on his bed kissing to…the rest. God, I could feel myself blush just thinking the words.

"Why me?" he said, the moment I'd shut the door behind me.

"Look at you," I said. He was propped up against his headboard with his shirt off—we'd gotten that far before I'd had to excuse myself for momentum-destroying sponge insertion. The twilight slanted in though the window, painting the planes of his lean, wiry frame with warm pink light and illuminating those insanely green eyes. His black hair fell in his face, and he swiped it away. Someone needed to paint *him*, for heaven's sake.

He ducked his head and actually looked embarrassed. Could I ever have imagined, back when he was snarling at me and I was trying to bribe him with pizza, that *I* could make *him* blush? It made me feel bold. Powerful.

"I'm no prize, Jenny," he said, meeting my eyes again.

"I'm not looking for a prize," I countered, reaching around and undoing the zipper that ran up the back of my dress with a confidence I was faking. I wasn't sure what I was looking for, in truth, but I didn't really care to parse it now. I just wanted to get out of my head. That part at least wasn't going to be hard, because just looking at him zoomed my body back to where it had been before, when we were kissing. A pulse began to beat between my legs, and as I let the dress fall and pool at my feet, the cool air hit my breasts, making my nipples peak almost painfully. I might have been a virgin, but I knew this feeling. I just hadn't known I could get so close without touching myself.

"God," he choked out, running his hands through his hair almost like he was having second thoughts.

I wasn't sure what to do with second thoughts. Had the onslaught of desire pressing down on me clouded my judgment? Had I made myself ridiculous? I pushed back at the questions. I didn't want them. They would only make me cautious, and that caution would hobble me. So I reached for the one word that made sense to me in that moment: "Matthew."

He was off the bed in a flash, hands grabbing my hips as he crashed his mouth down on mine. Once he had steadied me, his hands came up to my breasts, sliding up under the strapless bra I wore and tracing their undersides, all the while making wicked, deep incursions into my mouth with his tongue. I was on fire everywhere he touched. I was on fire everywhere, period.

And then, with no warning, he fell to his knees.

I knew what he was doing. I mean, I knew with my mind. I was acquainted with the act in theory. But that didn't mean I was prepared for him to shove my panties down around my knees and bury his face between my legs.

It also didn't mean I was able to stop myself from asking, on a shaky exhale, "What are you *doing*?" As I spoke, he darted a tongue out and licked me like I was an ice cream cone, sending a jolt of pleasure so strong through me that my question was followed by a moan. And I was sorry I'd asked it, because now, tilting his head up to meet my eyes, he was going to stop and answer me.

"I'm eating you out."

The matter-of-fact way he said it—oh, it did something to me. But part of me was still incredulous. "Why?"

"Because I want to." His eyes narrowed, almost like he was angry. But I'd seen him angry, and this wasn't that. "And judging by how wet you are, you do too. Am I wrong?"

"You're not wrong," I whispered.

So do you think you can shut the fuck up long enough for me to make you come?"

Oh, crap. His words alone almost did it. I had hoped I'd be able to shake off the heavy cloak of virginity I didn't want to wear anymore, but I had imagined it playing out more…traditionally. But now I wanted…this instead. So I nodded, not so much because I was obeying his command but because I no longer trusted my voice.

Matthew grabbed one of my buttocks with each hand to anchor himself, and apparently that initial lick had merely been an exploratory exercise, because, groaning, he sank his tongue into my folds. He set a rhythm of plunging in and out, licking me so intimately I should have been embarrassed, but I couldn't manage to do anything but gasp. With each stroke of his tongue, it was like a camera was gradually zooming in on the innermost part of me, making me heavy, saturated with sensation.

The fullness built and built until I thought I might not be able to stand it anymore. It was too much and, at the same time, not enough. Instinctively, I tried to buck my hips, but he tightened his grip on me, securing my butt with his forearms, all the while keeping up the wicked rhythm with his tongue. I was immobilized, pinned in place between his face and his arms, and I was so, so close. I let out a little sob of frustration.

He seemed to understand what it signified better than I did, because he lifted his face a little and swirled his tongue on my clit before pulling off long enough to rasp, "Is this what you want, Jenny?" Not waiting for an answer, he returned to my clit, taking it between his lips and sucking gently.

"Yes," I cried, grabbing his shoulders to keep from falling over.

A few seconds of suction, and I was shuddering and

trying to muffle my screams so I wouldn't wake his neighbors.

MATTHEW

I waited until she was done shaking, holding her tight with my arms wrapped around her middle—I was still kneeling—and willing myself not to come then and there. I had only known her a couple weeks, but I knew her well enough to know that in a minute, she'd become all flustered and embarrassed.

"Oh my God," she whispered.

There it was—not at all like the shouted invocations of the Lord that had been ripping from her throat earlier.

That was my cue. Because whatever else was going to happen, I didn't want her to be embarrassed. So, in a repeat of my earlier move, I flipped us both onto the bed, but this time I came down on top of her, bracing myself on my elbows as I kissed her breasts.

"That was—"

I whipped myself up and kissed her mouth. I didn't want to talk. Not yet. I just wanted to…savor this. Unlike at the construction site, there was no danger. No hurry. Nothing stopping us.

It sounded idiotic, but since it was her first time, I'd wanted to make sure she came. I wasn't schooled in the ways of virgins, but the conventional wisdom seemed to be that it could hurt the first time. And I didn't want to disappoint her. I'd almost made it through my time at this school without giving a shit about any of my fellow students or what they thought of me. Almost. So, yeah, I'd been…intent in my onslaught. I'd thought I'd been doing it for her, but honestly, ten seconds in, and nothing had ever turned me on more than torturing that girl with my tongue. And now I wanted to her to make those gutting mewling noises again. There had been something insanely hot about anchoring her pelvis, having her at my mercy while I'd worked her over.

But it turned out that a Jenny who was free to exert her will was pretty hot, too. Especially when her will seemed to involve wrapping her legs around my hips and clinging to me as if I were the art building in the path of the bulldozers.

"Oh my God, Matthew," she breathed, breaking the deep kiss she'd been planting on me. "I had no idea."

I grinned against her mouth. Honestly, I hadn't either. But I wasn't about to say that. So I bent to kiss my way down to her breasts. It suddenly seemed a crime that they had been so thoroughly neglected before, when I'd been on my knees. I took off her bra to reveal perfect handfuls of soft flesh, tipped by dark pink buds that I couldn't not put my mouth on.

She inhaled sharply, and I would have stopped to check that it was a happy inhale and not a distressed one, but she also bucked her hips, and since her legs were still wrapped around me, she lifted her whole pelvis off the bed and pressed it against my cock. It was like she was trying to angle me inside her.

"Will you do this already?" she pleaded.

I stopped everything, and her eyes, which had been half-closed, flew open. "Are you sure?" I asked.

She rolled her eyes.

I laughed. In that moment, she was so authentically herself, the Rainbow Brite-Jenny-journalist-crusader, that I couldn't help it.

"Yes," she said. "I'm sure." There was a tinge of impatience in her tone.

Or maybe it wasn't her tone. Maybe it was the hand that snaked down between our bodies and grabbed my dick.

I grunted, and she let go like it was on fire.

"Oh my God. Was that wrong? I've never touched one of those before."

I shook my head, trying not to laugh again. I wasn't laughing at her, but I didn't know how to explain it. I was laughing because it was either that or detonate.

So I slid in. I was inside Jenny, and it was like all her crazy colors were exploding inside *me* as she stretched to accommodate me. She was so tight. So slick. I stayed still for a moment, afraid that if I moved, we'd be done before we started. After a few breaths to gather myself, I started a slow rhythm, using one hand on her clit again. She must have still been sensitive from her orgasm because she winced when I made contact, but I persisted. She was trying to hold her head up, but after a minute of moving against each other, she gave up on a huge sigh and let her head fall back against the pillow as her eyes slipped closed.

I wished I could paint her like this. The sight of her, sprawled on my bed, naked, open to me...like the sun, it was almost too much to bear looking at, yet I wanted desperately to preserve the image forever.

She started holding her breath for little stretches, which was what she'd done last time just before she came, so I let myself slam into her, grinding hard when I was buried to the hilt and letting my own eyes close so I could submit to the torrent washing over me. I came to the edge, both relieved and resentful that it was about to be over. The last thing I remember, before I let the drowning happen, was Jenny exclaiming, wonder in her tone, "I'm going to come *again*!"

When it was over and I had swum back to the shore, heart pounding, chest heaving, she was quiet—*for once*. I didn't quite know what to do with that. But also, if she wasn't going to speak, I certainly didn't know what to say. I was afraid if we started talking, it would puncture this... balance we had achieved, and she would go back to her room. And whatever else happened, I didn't want her to encounter her shitty roommate tonight. Or, worse, Royce. The idea of Royce bothering her. The idea of Royce *looking* at her. No.

The silence that had settled wasn't an uncomfortable one, so I thought it was probably okay to just let it be. So I held her, her head on my chest, and listened to the sound of her breathing ratcheting down. The spaces between each inhale grew longer. Her body grew heavier. I could feel myself losing the battle against sleep, too. I didn't want to, though, not quite yet. So I gently eased her off my chest, praying she wouldn't wake up.

It was nearly dark. To think, the day had started with me drawing her, and ended with her shattering beneath me. It had started with me trying to blend the right colors to capture the ridiculous blue of her ridiculous dress, and now that ridiculous dress was wadded up on the floor of my room. I pulled the covers up over her, leaving only her face exposed to the dim extraneous light filtering in from the courtyard through the crack in the curtains. I'd always called her Rainbow Brite, but when she didn't have her fluffy, colorful clothes on, she was actually quite pale. Her lips, pink and plump against her porcelain skin, were the only shot of color on her tonight. It reminded me of a muted version of the woman on the Duran Duran cover.

I lowered my lips, placing them, feather-light, against hers.

The movement was gentle, measured, calculated not to startle her.

But the thought that whipped into my consciousness as I did so was the reverse: unexpected, unbidden, jarring.

I was made to kiss Jenny Fields.

CHAPTER SIX

JENNY

Well, I'd finally gotten my money's worth from the dress, I thought, grinning as I picked it up off the floor of Matthew's room and shimmied back into it while he slept. A slice of bright sunshine razored into the room where the curtains stood open a few inches. There were no clocks of any sort in his room, so I had no idea what time it was.

But I did know that I had to pee something fierce—not to mention get that sponge out. (*Please let the sponge have worked.*)

But no. I wasn't going to think about reality yet. Sponges and Nessa and Royce and the art building and graduation and Dad—none of it. When I reached the door to the bathroom, I pretended it was all those things and pushed them away as I straightened my arms to open it.

What if I just decided to ignore reality for a little while? I had never done that. I peed and got rid of the sponge. I didn't even say a prayer for its efficacy, because I decided that anxiety was part of the reality I was now officially on hiatus from. I gave myself a quick glance in the mirror, but who cared what I looked like, right? Reality: not interested. See? This was fun.

The one reality I couldn't escape was my morning breath, so, lacking a toothbrush, I swished with water as hot as I could stand and hoped for the best. Given the… amazingness of last night, I was pretty sure Matthew wasn't going to care.

Besides, I thought, unable to resist a little skip as I padded back down the hall to his room, I had learned that there were plenty of other places he could put his mouth. My face heated as the parts in question jumped to attention. My attraction to Matthew had been well established before last night. It was, in fact, why I had thrown the sponge in my bag when he called and asked if he could draw me. I hadn't assumed it would happen, but a part of me had hoped it would.

And when it had…dear God, I'd had *no idea*.

I had been thinking of my virginity like a cast that had come off. I didn't want it anymore, and sex was what I had to do to saw it off. It wasn't that I'd been expecting it to be unpleasant. I just hadn't known it was possible for someone to be so tender and deliciously rough at the same time. So solicitous yet ravenous. My whole body tingled from the memory. My poor, poor body had had a taste of what was possible and, I feared, was never going to let me forget it.

I stood with my hands pressed against another door, the door to Matthew's room. I had no idea what was going to happen, but I knew one thing with certainty. This time I didn't want to push anything away. I didn't even want to fix anything. I didn't want to talk about what he was going to do after graduation. At this moment, I didn't even care about the art building. (*I didn't care about the art building!*)

I just wanted more of the person who had made me feel this way, like reality was just an inconvenience to be postponed for later. So I pushed open the door that stood between us.

He was bent over, pulling on his jeans, and disappointment cut through me. But it was probably late. He probably had to be in class.

"Hey," I ventured, not even trying to temper the grin I could feel splaying across my face. God, to look at that bare, gently sculpted chest. At those arms and hands, so capable of so many things: punching Royce, drawing something so beautiful it hurt, bringing me to orgasm. To have them displayed like that, like I had enough ownership to see him so casually bared, made my stomach flutter.

He looked up, finished pulling up his jeans, and straightened, echoing my greeting. "Hey." There was no answering smile as he turned and began stuffing things into his backpack. "So, I gotta get to the studio," he said, still facing away from me. "I have an appointment with my mentor for my senior portfolio later today." When he finally stopped messing with his backpack, he had to turn around—there was no way for him to not look at me as he left the room. But the face that turned back to me wore a neutral, bland expression. Not angry or upset. Just... empty. Not the way I imagined a guy should look at a girl when he'd spent a good portion of time the night before with his face between her legs. Or forget that, even—what about the drawings? The confrontation at the pub? The cartoon? Was that all just...gone?

"Right." I blinked several times in succession, willing the tears that were gathering to dissipate. I knew I was being blown off. It wasn't like I thought we'd become girlfriend and boyfriend. Not necessarily, anyway. I started to say something to that effect, to reassure him. But I swallowed the words before they could escape, adding them to the bitter lump forming in my throat. Because to say something like that sounded desperate, implied that I had entertained the notion long enough to dismiss it.

But I had. That was the horrible truth I could never admit to anyone. I'd been pushing away reality because I hadn't wanted to overthink things. I hadn't wanted to *ruin* things. I'd decided for one second in my life to just let myself be. But the problem with exorcising reality was that the thing that replaced it was fantasy. Matthew and Jenny, the unlikely couple, striding across campus hand in hand. Me bringing him food. Watching him paint. Publishing his cartoons.

Falling asleep in his arms.

Fantasy. It was, by definition, false. It floated away on the wind.

And once it was gone, it left a vacuum. And what do they say? Nature abhors a vacuum? It must be true, because once fantasy is gone, reality comes whooshing back in, violently filling all the space available to it, clattering up against your insides.

There was nothing left to do but try to save face. I looked around the room and spotted a shoe. As I bent to collect it, he said, "Take your time."

I glanced up. Had I misinterpreted him saying he had to go to the studio?

"If you can just turn the lock on the doorknob before you shut it behind you, that would be great."

No. I had read the situation correctly. He was going to leave, and he wasn't even going to wait two minutes for me to get my stuff together. He couldn't get away from me fast enough. I didn't trust my voice, so I just nodded. This was what happened when you didn't plan, when you shoved reality aside: you weren't prepared for heartbreak when it came crashing down on you like an anvil falling from the sky in an old-fashioned cartoon.

He paused with his hand on the doorknob and cleared his throat. "See you."

He didn't wait for my reaction, which was good, because he didn't see me start to cry.

MATTHEW

The thing is, I had never kissed anybody before without getting something out of it. It had always been a prelude to something else. Not a bargaining chip, per se. I wasn't *that* calculating. But, in the past, kisses had always been... transactional. The first act in a longer production. Not ends in themselves.

I was made to kiss Jenny Fields. That had been the thought drifting through my mind last night as I succumbed to sleep. As unlikely as the situation was—as unlikely as *she* was—I hadn't been able to stop myself from pressing my mouth against her petal-pink lips.

But in the harsh light of day, I could not ignore the question that followed: why? Why on earth would I have bothered kissing someone who wasn't even awake to feel it?

And as I laid there, pretending to be asleep but peeking at her as she struggled into her dress and slipped out of my room—her bare feet signaling that she was only headed for the bathroom, and not, as my cowardly heart had hoped, actually leaving—I forced myself to confront the truth: I knew what that rib-cracking feeling last night had been.

And that was *not* happening.

I'd been on my knees before her, for fuck's sake. Rainbow Brite had literally brought me to my knees.

And I could not afford that kind of distraction. The end was in sight, if I could just wrangle Curry and this senior project. I hadn't been working myself to the bone for nearly four years to go soft just before the finish line. And that was what Rainbow Brite made me: soft. Soft wasn't going to get me where I needed to be. Soft was unacceptable. As I stalked across campus, shaky and starving, self-disgust flowed through me. Maybe it would freeze the weakness out of me, harden the lava I'd imagined Jenny pouring through me last night, leaving me strong and unbendable.

As I yanked open the huge, heavy oak door to the art building to get my drawings before I caught the bus into the city, I paused, breathing heavily, and physically rested my forehead against the wood. This door was more than a hundred years old. The thought was oddly grounding. Calming. The door never changed. It had acquired the patina of age, of course, its scrapes and nicks marking the march of years. But it hadn't changed fundamentally. Hard and difficult to move, it was immune to the generations of students, to their dramas, to the passage of something as insignificant as time.

After a few more deep breaths, the panic began to loosen its hold on my gut enough that I was able to make my way to the studio to fetch the drawings I would bring to Curry. I packed quickly, averting my eyes from the images as I slid them into a portfolio. By the time I pushed against the building's front door again, I was composed. Solid, like the door. Made of strong, unbreakable wood.

CHAPTER SEVEN

JENNY

It was days like this I wished Dad wasn't so far away. It wasn't that I expected him ever to get his shit together enough that I could confide in him so he could comfort me. (Besides, I don't think even fathers who are paragons of mental health want to hear about how their daughters gave it up to a boy who turned out to be a total jerkface.) But sometimes I envied students whose families lived close enough that they could go home for the weekend. Because right about now, climbing into my childhood bed, pulling the covers over my head, and hiding from the world long enough to get my self back without everyone's eyes on me sounded like heaven.

I took a deep breath at the door to my room and tried to tell myself that facing Nessa couldn't be worse than the hateful version of Matthew I'd encountered earlier. Part of me hoped she wouldn't be there. But it was probably better to get it over with. I had resolved to tell her about Royce. Then we'd have to find a way to get on. It was too close to the end of the year to expect housing services to reassign us, but if worse came to worst, I could crash at Tony's off-campus apartment, assuming he wasn't entertaining one of his legions of female admirers.

Just as I was about go to the door, it opened from the inside.

I jumped, and so did Nessa.

Then she threw her arms around me and started crying.

It hadn't been nearly as hard as I'd anticipated to tell Nessa about my scary encounter with Royce at freshman orientation. I had expected her to be angry, and she was, but not in the way I'd been braced for. I'd prepared myself for her to be defensive, to not believe me, to take Royce's part.

But instead, after informing me that she'd broken up with Royce the night before, she started laying into me about not telling her earlier. "I don't even mean once I started dating him, Jenny. Like, earlier-earlier. Why have you been carrying this around for three and a half years without talking to anyone?"

I shrugged. "I dunno. He just grabbed my boobs. It's not like he—"

"Don't make excuses for him. *God.* I'm such a dipstick." She'd been sitting next to me on my bed, but she stood and walked over to her own and gave her pillow a hearty *thwack*. "Ugh! I wish I could hit him."

"Well, actually…" I said, grinning at the memory of Matthew decking Royce, even though thinking about Matthew at all was sort of like taking a razor blade to my heart. I hadn't been planning to tell her about Matthew.

But then, I hadn't been expecting the old Nessa, the one who was funny and smart and sympathetic and *not brainwashed*. So it all came out.

She was hugging me again by the time I was done with my tale of woe. "I'm sorry," she whispered, sitting on my bed and holding me in her arms while I cried.

I shrugged. "I wanted to lose my virginity."

"Not about that. Well, I *am* sorry about that. But I meant I'm sorry I pretty much abandoned you this year. I feel like if I had been…more present, maybe none of this stuff with Matthew would have happened."

I shook my head. "I abandoned you too. I hate myself for not telling you about Royce earlier. I feel like I let you walk into the lion's den with no warning." The guilt was stronger than ever now that I had my old friend back. What had been *wrong* with me? How could I not have warned her?

"It wouldn't have mattered," she said. "Lots of people told me he was bad news. Like Dawn Hathaway—if anyone should know, it would be the gossip columnist, right? But I didn't listen. I was determined to be with him."

"Why?" I asked, as gently as I could.

"I'm not as strong as you, Jenny. I mean, who am I? I get B-minuses. I never talk in class. I'm the production coordinator of the newspaper. You know why I went for that job?"

It had never occurred to me to ask. "Why?"

"Because when you're production coordinator, you don't have to go out into the world and ask people questions. You just have to make sure everything's running smoothly."

"It's an important job," I protested.

"I didn't say it wasn't. But it's also an invisible job."

I sighed. I got it. "And then Royce takes notice, and suddenly you're not invisible anymore."

"The parties, the beautiful people, the gifts. It was a whirlwind." She shook her head, clearly frustrated with herself. "And the truth is, I didn't want to resist. I wanted to…pretend for a while." Her voice caught. "Even though, somewhere in my heart, I knew it wasn't real."

It was my turn to hug her. We sat like that for a while; then she sniffed and pulled away, flashing me a crooked smile. "You know what? I'm kind of wondering now if he pursued me because of you."

"How so?" I asked, though I knew full well what she meant.

"He talked about you all the time. It was almost like he was obsessed with you." She cocked her head and stared at the ceiling for a moment. "You know, I met him at that frat party in September. You remember? The Delta Chi back-to-school bash? You took Beth home early because she was sick."

I did remember. The youngest member of the newspaper had miscalibrated a bit on her first big college party, and I'd felt responsible for her. Ironically, I hadn't wanted Royce to get her in his sights. I couldn't have imagined my roommate would roll in hours later, aflutter because she'd kissed the guy and he was taking her sailing that weekend.

"I knew Royce, of course," said Nessa. We all did. You didn't go to Allenhurst without knowing its golden boy, at least by reputation. "But I'd never spoken a word to him in three years. But that night, right after you left with Beth, he came up to me and asked if I knew you. He had seen us talking earlier. I told him we'd been roommates since the beginning." She huffed a bitter laugh. "And then he asked me out."

God. It only confirmed my suspicions, but I felt terrible for Nessa, grappling not only with the news that her boyfriend was a horrible person, but that he had been using her this whole time. "Yeah, I don't think anyone has ever told Royce 'no' before. I feel like maybe he *has* been a little obsessed with me. Not because he likes me, but because…" It was hard to explain.

"He feels like you owe him something."

I nodded. "I'm sorry."

"Enough sorry!" Nessa waved her hands in a dismissive motion. "Enough boys, too!"

"I'll second that motion," I said, smiling sadly.

"Let's go to Boston." She stood and held out her hand. "Just you and me, like we used to. If we leave now, we can be there by lunch."

We did used to make the ninety-minute bus ride to the city every couple of months, to see a Red Sox game or go shopping or just to hang out in some new scenery. We hadn't been all year. I was exhausted, but…

I took her hand. "That is an offer I cannot refuse."

MATTHEW

Curry didn't say anything for a really long time as he circled the portraits of Jenny. He didn't light a second cigarette when the first one burned down.

"You are in love with this girl." It wasn't a question.

"*What*? No!" I had to take a step back, I was so stunned by the pronouncement.

He narrowed his eyes at me and then looked back at the drawings. "Perhaps you hate her then?"

"I don't *hate* her," I said, realizing too late that it came out sounding awfully defensive—the artist doth protest too much and all that.

My maddening mentor shrugged, as if it were all the same to him. "These are the best I've ever seen from you. You're finally getting somewhere."

"Because I cranked out some pastels of some chick?" I probably shouldn't have been talking to him like that, but I couldn't help it.

"You are torturing yourself over this woman." He smirked. Before I could muster a protest, he added, "It is not necessary to torture yourself to make great art." He held up a finger, as if to forestall the rejoinder he thought was coming, but in truth, I was too shocked to speak. "But if you're going to do it, better over a woman than something that doesn't matter."

"I only met her a couple weeks ago, so—"

"Torture yourself over a woman," he continued, as if I hadn't spoken at all. "That's understandable. You can use that. But the rest of it? You've been torturing yourself about everything all semester. Form. Technique. God knows what else." He turned to me. It was still so strange to see him without his trademark cigarette. "And how has that been working out for you?"

"Suffering has nothing to do with art?" I shot back. "What about Van Gogh? Bacon? Arbus?" My voice rose, indignant, because he was wrong.

"Some artists manage to leverage their suffering into greatness. But suffering isn't a precondition to great art, Matthew. Caring is, though. You can't just be a robot the rest of your life. You have to let yourself care about something."

It was the most he had ever said to me in one go. We stared at each other for a long time. How could this asshole presume to know anything about me? About whether I'd suffered. About whether my suffering was *worthy*. About what I'd had to do to get through the past four years. About what I'd had to do to get through the last *twenty-two*.

"What I care about," I finally whispered, shaking so hard with suppressed rage that I couldn't make my voice any louder, "is not flunking out of college. What I care about is my goddamned senior portfolio."

Curry smiled as he stared at me. Seeing him smile was even weirder than seeing him without a cigarette. "I don't give a flying fuck about your senior portfolio, Townsend. You do what you like, and I'll sign off on it."

Then he turned and lit a cigarette, dismissing me.

It wasn't late enough when I got back to campus. It wasn't *dark* enough, the spring days having grown longer without me noticing. That I was planning to go out without sufficient darkness was a sign of how out of control I was. But I was beyond caring. I banged into my room and yanked the portraits of Jenny out of my portfolio. When I ripped the corner of one of them, it only fanned the flames of my rage. I didn't even have a new stencil, for fuck's sake. It showed how utterly distracted I'd let myself become in recent weeks. I slammed my backpack on my bed, intending to empty it so I could refill it with my supplies, but the already-wobbly zipper finally gave way, and all my shit went flying.

Fuck it. I didn't need the backpack. I just had to go, had to obey the fire in my limbs commanding that I *keep moving*. I grabbed a garbage bag, jerked my closet door open, threw all my paint cans into the bag, and headed out into the twilight.

I could feel the fury starting to dissipate as I walked. It was like my junkie body knew it was going to get its fix soon, and it opened a tiny pinhole in my chest, allowing the rage that had accumulated there to begin to hiss out. By the time I was done, a couple hours from now, I would be okay, back to myself. I glanced at the art building up ahead. I'd be that goddamned wooden door, unchanging and impermeable.

The art building sat at one end of a circular commons that formed the center of campus. It was lined with the university's oldest, most stately buildings, anchored by Salter Tower, the college's iconic clock tower, and ringed by a roundabout used by buses coming into campus. As I approached, a regional commuter bus of the same variety from which I had recently disembarked pulled up in front of the student center, which was on the opposite side of the circle from the art building. I slowed my pace and averted my face. Some of the profs commuted to campus from Boston, and though it was unlikely that any of them would be arriving on a Sunday evening, I had to make sure no one with any authority saw me leaving campus with my sketchy garbage bag. As the bus pulled away, I allowed myself to glance over to see if I needed to worry about any of the passengers.

One. There was one I needed to worry about.

She was laughing, laden with shopping bags and

jokingly objecting to something that Nessa was saying. She was back in her colorful armor: a denim miniskirt, purple leggings, and a matching loose purple T-shirt belted low across her waist.

The pinhole that had opened up in my chest ripped itself into a huge, gaping rift, and instead of exiting in an orderly, drawn-out fashion, my rage was all sucked out of me in one heaving, horrible instant.

You have to let yourself care about something.

The shocking truth was that I wanted to fall to my knees before her once again. Right now and every day for the rest of my life. So I could taste her, yes, but also so I could beg the forgiveness I came nowhere near to deserving. So I could exhort her to have me.

"Was I drunk to let you talk me into that?" Jenny exclaimed, looping her arm through her roommate's. "Because I am never going to wear that shirt."

"Shut up! That shirt is amazing! You're going to kill in it."

"It doesn't even have a back, Ness! It—"

Even if I hadn't been watching them, standing there immobilized by the great roiling mass of fear and love and anguish and lust and guilt that had taken up residence inside me, I would have been able to pinpoint the exact moment she saw me. It was the moment the laughing, teasing, easygoing banter died. Killed by the sight of a boy who had broken her. Or tried to. Because even if she didn't know it herself, no one could ever really break her.

Her face took only a moment to catch up with what she was seeing. Then it rid itself of all outward sign of emotion. Like the door. The untouchable door. Oh God, it was like being lanced directly in the heart. Rainbow Brite wasn't supposed to look like that. To *be* like that—

immovable and impenetrable. She deserved so much better.

So why, said a little voice inside my head, didn't I think I did, too?

I watched Nessa take in the scene. She used the arm that was already linked with Jenny's to pull her friend closer and began marching down the sidewalk. They'd been headed my direction, but Nessa rerouted them, sending them the long way around the circle so they wouldn't have to pass me. When they were a good ten yards away, Nessa looked over her shoulder at me. I couldn't hear, but I could read her lips clear as day: "Asshole."

Jenny, by contrast, did not look back.

I had to fix this. I had to fix a lot of things.

I made for the art building. There was that door again. What the hell? Why had I assigned so much bullshit symbolism to it? I dropped my bag and pressed both hands against the wood, like I wanted to make sure it had no miraculous powers. Nope. Just a fucking door.

Which I pushed open, a new mission crystallized in my head. I needed to find someone with a camera.

CHAPTER EIGHT

JENNY

I woke the next morning to pounding. At first, I thought it was just my head, because after seeing Matthew on the circle, Nessa had taken me straight to a bar—not the one Matthew worked at—and gotten me drunk, and we'd stumbled home after last call.

But it hadn't been enough. I had wanted to forget him, just for one night. To numb myself. But it hadn't been possible. My mind couldn't let go of the images assaulting it. It was the contrast between them that slayed me. Him laughing as we fell together onto his bed. Him kissing me like he would die if he stopped. Then, just as vivid: him staring at me as I got off the bus, wearing that same, horrible, blank expression he'd turned on me earlier that morning. As if he didn't even *know* me.

But as Nessa stumbled toward the door, groaning—she'd had her own heartbreak to nurse last night, after all—I realized the pounding was coming from outside.

"What?" she snapped, opening the door. Then her voice softened. "Tony?"

"You have to come," he said, barging into the room, aiming the order at me.

"I'm not going anywhere today, Tony," I said, turning over to face the wall. "Tell Beth to run the editorial meeting." I'd been planning on recommending to the paper's board that Beth get the editor-in-chief job next year, so it couldn't hurt for her to get some experience now.

"Jenny, get out of bed," he said. "There's something you need to see."

Something about the tone the usually mild-mannered photographer used to deliver his directive got me out of bed. I sent him outside to wait while I threw on some sweats and brushed my teeth. Just like two mornings ago in the bathroom at Matthew's dorm, I didn't look in the mirror. I didn't want to see what he had reduced me to.

"I was in the darkroom late last night," Tony explained as he and Nessa and I set off across the quad, "when the door opened."

Nessa looked at me warily. I knew what she was thinking: Royce.

"It was that Matthew Townsend kid."

"What?" Nessa said, her voice indignant.

"Yeah, and he ruined an entire box of photo paper."

"What did he want?" I couldn't help it. I wanted to not care what Matthew did, but if Tony didn't keep telling the story, I would drag it out of him.

I needn't have worried, because obviously whatever happened had been weighing on Tony, and he was anxious to unburden himself. He wrung his hands as he walked. "He begged me to help him with his senior portfolio. He said he had all the art done—installations, he said. He just needed someone to walk around with him and take photos to document them."

I sucked in a breath. He couldn't mean... "The graffiti?" I whispered.

"Yeah," said Tony. He's the guy whose been doing all that political graffiti all these years. And his stuff—it's amazing."

So why was Tony so worked up? He didn't know about Matthew and me.

"So we walked around," he continued. "It wasn't quite dark yet, so we got some good shots. There was more to do when night really fell, so we walked back to the circle and parted ways there, agreeing that we'd meet at the art building this morning to photograph the rest."

"It was nice of you to help him," I offered weakly, not sure what else to say.

"I did it for you."

"Excuse me?"

"Well, for the art building," he clarified. "I thought if I did him a favor, maybe I could get him to use any pull he had with the department, or that Curry guy, to protest the demolition."

Tears sprang to my eyes. Why couldn't I have fallen for a guy like Tony? He was a Goth, which was not at all my type, and came off as kind of a playboy, but he was always doing these sweet, thoughtful things.

"But, really, once I saw what he was doing, it felt, like...important to help him." He seemed anguished, like he was apologizing to me for something.

"I know." I nodded, feeling like he needed me to dispense absolution for some reason I couldn't understand. "His work could be really significant if he would just... allow it to be."

"Well, I'm exposing the film when I get back to my room," Tony said angrily as we rounded the corner that would put us onto the circle. He'd taken us along a path that came up along the side of the art building and deposited us right in front of it.

Nessa saw it before I did and gasped. I looked at her first, saw the horror on her face as she clasped a hand over her mouth.

"I'm sorry," Tony said. "I thought you should see it. I'm going to leave you here and go get some of the newspaper people together to see about getting it removed." He patted my arm awkwardly and left.

I let my eyes slide over the lettering, biting down on the inside of my cheeks to keep from wailing.

FOR A GOOD TIME, CALL JENNY. 867-5309.

In gold spray paint.

You're basically never going to see gold graffiti.

"Let's go," said Nessa, tugging on my arms. But I planted my feet. I couldn't stop looking at it. "You've seen it," she added. "So please, let's just go."

"He didn't even make it look good." In some ways, that was the bigger blow. He could create the most stunning works of art, was capable of such breathtaking, exacting work, even when in a hurry, as I had witnessed when we'd done the Reagan *Star Wars* piece together. But these were crude letters that looked like a kid had drawn them.

But perhaps that was intentional. Crude letters to match the crude sentiment.

"How could I have been so wrong about him?" I whispered, recognizing even as I spoke the words that they had been a feminine chorus since time immemorial. I'd chosen him because I thought he was different. More evolved. But he was no better than Royce.

The very worst part about all of this was that he had made me question not just my romantic judgment, but *everything* about myself. Could I ever trust myself again? And if not, how was I ever going to have the guts to move to New York and will my way into a career I now wasn't sure I was constitutionally capable of? An investigative journalist had to have, above all things, good judgment. She had to be able to trust her intuition.

He had taken that from me, too. He had taken everything that mattered.

"I need to get out of this school," I said, though I wasn't sure to whom I was speaking.

"Just a month left," Nessa said. Then she took my hand and squeezed it. "Three weeks of class. That's six more newspapers. Then some exams. Then you're free."

The pressure on my hand and the truth of the words functioned like anchors. Something to hold onto while a hurricane raged around me—and inside me. She was right. I couldn't let him have everything. I had my friends. I had the newspaper—and Dawn had a huge story brewing that was going to run in the last issue of the school year. It was going to cause a lot of controversy, and I needed to make sure my head was in the game.

I nodded. Nessa, the eye of my storm, wrapped her arms around me and gave me a quick, fierce hug. Then she tugged my arm again, and this time I let her lead me away.

What else could I do except start counting the days?

MATTHEW

I hadn't seen it because I had been in Boston. My plan had been to meet Tony as we'd agreed the night before. I was going to try to badger him into developing all the film right after we got back from our second outing, and then take it to Curry.

But in the end, once I had decided, I couldn't wait.

You have to let yourself care about something.

I'd hopped the 6 a.m. Boston bus and gone to Curry's house, where I pounded on his door until he woke up and answered it, cursing and smoking simultaneously.

"And why didn't you go to this girl first?" Curry asked as we cruised down the highway back toward Allenhurst in his late-model BMW. For all the ramshackle shabbiness of his studio, it seemed he did pretty well. "Why didn't you follow her last night after you saw her get off the bus?"

I had told him everything—about the graffiti and about Jenny. Because it was all mixed up so badly there was no point in trying to untangle it. If I had decided to do what Curry said and finally care about something, it was because of her. Because she made me not need to go out and do graffiti to feel okay. Which was confusing, because I was trying to argue to Curry that the graffiti should be my senior portfolio.

"I needed to get my shit figured out first," I said. "I didn't want to come to her all…damaged. Without having changed anything."

"Because from my vantage point, it sort of looks like you're leaving her hanging while you fart around with your senior portfolio."

I could see how it looked that way. What I wasn't telling him was that I was going to move to New York when I graduated. I hoped with Jenny, but even if she wouldn't have me, I'd go. But first I needed to show her—

and myself—that I could do something that mattered. That I had a *reason* to move to New York and say, "I am an artist."

Curry razzed me pretty well all the way back to Allenhurst. But then when I took him to the first site and he got out of the car, he shut up. "And you're saying there's more?" he asked, turning to me.

I almost laughed. "So much more."

"Well, let's go, then."

After we'd been to a dozen or so sites, we headed back to the art building. He hadn't spoken much during his perusal of my vandalism-turned-art, but on the way back to the car he insisted that we find Tony and get him to develop the film he'd already taken. He was even talking about hiring a professional to shoot the rest. "Although we *could* just ask your goddamned advisor to meet us in one of your alleys." He snickered.

I didn't know whether to laugh, because I didn't know if he was serious. I didn't know if he knew that my "goddamned advisor" would do whatever Curry told him to do.

We parked in a lot a block or so away from the art building, and as we approached, I saw a small crowd of people gathered, and I could hear them buzzing, though I couldn't make out any of what they were saying. My heart leapt, because what else could it be but some kind of protest led by Jenny?

My body ached for her. I wanted to see her so badly, yet I clung stubbornly to the notion that I needed to sort out the portfolio first. I needed to do what both she and Curry had been telling me to do. I needed to become the sort of man who was worthy of her.

"Oh, look, here's her little fagboy boyfriend."

Unfortunately, I would have known that voice anywhere. I looked around, trying to spot Jenny or Nessa or any of the newspaper people. But it was all frat-boy types in their baggy khakis and pink shirts with upturned collars like they were dressed for cricket or polo or some shit.

"Royce," I said as the crowd parted and opened a path between me and him. I wasn't afraid of him. Curry's presence helped, but mostly, I stood straight and proud in the private knowledge that, no matter how terribly and possibly irrevocably I'd bungled things, for one crystalline moment, Jenny had chosen *me*. Royce would never be able to say that.

He just sneered and glanced over his shoulder. I followed his gaze, and—

No. No, no, no.

"No." I said it out loud, as if that would somehow change what I was seeing.

The bag. I'd dropped the bag yesterday, after Jenny got off the bus and I'd been annihilated by the truth of how fucking much I loved her. For some moronic reason, I'd become momentarily obsessed with touching the door to the art building and I'd needed to free up my hands.

And, I only now realized, I'd never picked up the goddamned bag again.

It wasn't just the ugly sentiment, but the fact that he'd painted it on her beloved art building. He might as well have spit in her face.

This couldn't stand. Something shifted inside me, and it must have been reflected in my outward being, because Royce flinched, and as he did so, a murmur rippled through the crowd. He thought I was going to hit him, but he was wrong. I held his gaze a moment longer, but I wasn't even tempted. I was done with Royce.

I swiveled to face Curry. "Change of plans." He raised his eyebrows. "I have something I need to do, but I can't do it by myself. I need help. Will you help me?"

Jesus, if only he knew how hard it was to choke those words past the fear lodged in my throat.

One end of his mouth quirked up slightly. Maybe he *did* know. "I thought you'd never ask." Then the other side hitched up too. "I have no idea what you have in mind, but I think I might need to go back to the car for my cigarettes."

JENNY

Enough with the pounding already. I was taking a nap. Well, I was *trying* to take a nap. Nessa, having capitulated to my insistence that she go oversee the production of tomorrow's paper, had extracted from me a promise that I would try to sleep. Ever dutiful, I was lying on my bed in the dark. My head felt less awful than it had earlier, but that was about all I could say for myself. The only reason I'd succumbed to Nessa's demand was that I knew promising to rest was the only thing that would get her out of the room. Though I appreciated the loyalty, I wanted to be alone so I could cry. And I had. Cried until I felt like an empty shell. Like he'd broken not just my heart but my lungs and guts and marrow, too.

"Jenny!" called the voice at my door. "Jenny, it's Beth! Open the door!"

I groaned. Beth was supposed to be overseeing the planning for Thursday's paper. I had thought she was the type who could rise to the occasion and not need hand-holding, but apparently I was wrong.

I heaved myself out of my cocoon and hobbled over to swing open the door. "What's wrong?"

"I tried to call, but it keeps ringing and ringing."

I rolled my eyes. "Yeah, well, I had to take the phone off the hook." The phone had been ringing when Nessa and I got back to the room earlier, and after answering it and listening for a few seconds, Nessa had slammed it down without speaking. A couple more repeats of that, and she pulled the whole thing out of the wall before tucking me in.

"You have to come with me!" Beth urged.

God, would everyone just stop with this today?

"The art building! You have to see it!" She was breathless, far from her usual no-nonsense self.

"I've seen it, Beth. Why else do you think I'm holed up here wallowing in my misery? Why else is my phone off the hook?" If she was only just now finding out, she wasn't the newswoman I'd believed her to be.

"You haven't seen *this*." She came into the room and flipped on the overhead light, leaving me blinking and holding my head. She made a slow turn around the room until she spied my pink hoodie. She picked it up off the floor and threw it at me. "Put this on. We're going."

What the hell? It couldn't get any worse.

"What are you putting on the front page on Thursday?" I asked as I followed her toward the center of campus. Man, she was going fast.

"I'm putting *this* on the front page."

I wanted to protest, but I couldn't. The graffiti was certain to be big news on campus. "I'm surprised it's still up," I said, thinking of Tony's promise that he'd get rid of it. Several hours had passed since I'd parted from him.

She shot me a look. "So you *do* know about it?" When, confused, I didn't answer, she said, "Anyway, I'm not sure it will be there much longer. The administration is out there. President Bannister is talking to Curry."

Emmanuel Curry? What the hell?

A huge crowd was assembled on the circle. Some of them carried hand-lettered placards exhorting the administration to save the art building. As we walked, an ABC news truck from the Boston affiliate pulled up.

"Whoa," said Beth. "This shit is getting real. I hope Tony is getting this." She started looking around the crowd, which, despite my confusion, gave me some measure of comfort. At least my heir was comporting herself with the concern befitting an editor facing a situation that…

What the heck was actually happening here? The crowd was so thick that I couldn't see what everyone was looking at.

"Oh my God!" an unfamiliar voice cried. "I think that's the girl."

"Jenny!" I turned because that second voice, coming from behind me, was one I recognized.

"Nessa!" I called as she ran toward me, huffing heavily. "What's happening?"

"I tried to find you—I've just come from our room."

"Why?" I was getting impatient. "Will someone please tell me what's going on?"

She took my hand and started barking, "Excuse us, make way, please," as she elbowed her way through the crowd. When we encountered a particularly thick clump, she snapped, "This is the girl from the painting, so make way."

Those seemed to be the magic words, because a path opened, and Nessa dropped my hand and gave me a shove.

I stumbled forward a bit but managed to right myself.

"Walk," she hissed.

So I did what any good journalist would have: I walked.

I saw him before I saw what he was doing. He was perched on a not-super-reliable-looking scaffolding, and my first thought was that he was going to hurt himself. He had to be twenty feet up, and he was reaching as far as he could with a paintbrush and—

Oh my God.

It was me. He was painting me.

It was the same image from one of the pastel drawings from the other morning—the sad one. It was huge, though, taking up nearly a third of the wall. He'd already finished my face, which was how I could tell it was the sad one. The hair was done, and he was working on the place where my shoulder met my blue dress. There was a second scaffolding maybe twenty feet over from him, and someone had clearly used it to paint SAVE THE ART BUILDING in letters that were maybe three feet high. They'd been hand-lettered but they were perfectly aligned, so immaculate one would have thought they'd been type-written. Beneath them was a numbered list, done in smaller letters. I took a step closer. The first said, "This building is over a hundred years old, and the only example of Gothic revival architecture on campus." There were three more items in the list, but it appeared that it wasn't finished. I didn't think Matthew had done the lettering. It seemed impossible that he could have done as much of the painting as he had and made this list in the hours that had elapsed since I'd been here and seen my phone number—which was now nowhere in evidence.

I looked around. There was an older man standing in paint-splattered jeans and a T-shirt, and he was talking to President Bannister and a couple other men, one of whom I recognized as the chair of the university's board of governors.

"You have to understand, Mr. Curry—"

"What the hell does it matter what he paints on it if you're going to tear it down anyway?" Curry yelled, waving a paintbrush that confirmed his identity as Matthew's partner in crime.

"Jenny." I turned, wary, no idea what or who to expect. What could this day possibly have left to serve up to me?

"Officer Artie!" I smiled despite myself. Officer Perez and I had had our clashes over the years, but right now he seemed like a friendly, reliable face in a crowd I still wasn't sure how to classify.

He glanced at the argument unfolding between Curry and the president. "I'm not sure how much longer this"—he gestured at Matthew's scaffolding—"will be allowed to go on."

I nodded. "I'm not going to chain myself to the front door or anything, so don't worry."

He smiled. "No. I just thought you might want to…I don't know. Go up there and talk to him?"

"You're telling me to go ahead and climb that rickety-ass-looking scaffolding up to where a student is committing a crime in broad daylight?"

"I'm not telling you to do that," he said. "I'm just

telling you if you *were* going to do something like that, you might want to get to it."

He winked and went over to insert himself into the escalating argument between the men.

I walked to the base of Matthew's scaffolding. It was amazing. There were probably three hundred people milling around at his feet. Emmanuel Curry was defending Matthew's guerrilla art project—vociferously— with the school's top brass. Matthew was hanging precariously twenty feet in the sky. Yet none of these things seemed to penetrate his consciousness at all. He worked with a single-minded intensity that made me blush because it reminded me of the way he had gone down on me.

Did I dare?

I dared.

MATTHEW

I didn't notice her until she was right there. Which, come to think of it, was a pretty good metaphor for our entire relationship. I'd been fine for nearly four years, content in my complete ignorance of the existence of Jenny Fields. If I had seen her from afar, I would have classified her as of a type: rich, preppy, entitled.

But then she was just…there. In my space and in my face. And once she was there, it was impossible that she should be anywhere else.

Our eyes met as her head popped up over the floor of the scaffolding I stood on. I went to her, grabbing her arm as she hoisted herself up the last rung of the ladder, because I was suddenly seized with fear that she would fall.

But I dropped her arm as soon as she stood before me, safe and upright. I didn't have the right to touch her anymore.

But I could speak the truth.

You have to let yourself care about something.

"I love you," I said, and, amazingly, I wasn't afraid.

"What?" She laughed, but it was a nervous, unsettled laugh, not her usual delighted, conspiratorial giggle.

"I love you."

She furrowed her brow. She was skeptical, and rightly so.

What did I think? That I could just keep saying it and it would somehow make a difference? That it would be enough? I tried another truth. "I didn't paint your phone number on the wall." The little intake of breath that followed told me I was getting somewhere. "I dropped a bag with my paint in it near here last night. Someone else must have picked it up."

"Royce," she breathed.

"Seems likely," I agreed.

"So what *are* you doing?" She gestured to the building.

I turned back to the work I was creating—the work *we* were creating, Curry and me. It was looking okay. I'd chosen to reproduce the sad version of her, because I thought it seemed more appropriate to the destruction of a building. I'd taped the original to the bricks near my feet and was doing a half-decent job copying it. And who knew Curry would be content to lower himself to lettering the text I'd given him? Except he wasn't lettering right now. He seemed to be arguing with a bunch of old dudes who looked like they were in charge. I couldn't hear anything the suits were saying, but Curry was yelling, and phrases like "protest art" and "artistically illiterate corporate BS" were wafting up.

Crap—this might actually work.

"What I am doing," I said, going back to Jenny's question, "is trying to get this piece-of-shit school to spare this old pile of bricks."

She smiled then, as she stood there in her neon-pink sweatshirt and lime-green leggings. "I knew you cared about this place underneath all that bravado."

"Actually, I don't give a fuck about the art building." I had looked her in the eyes and told her the truth when I said I loved her, and now I couldn't seem to stop. The truth was addicting. "I've told you that. I'm just doing this for you. Because I love you." I smiled. "As I said."

She covered her face with her hands, and a little sob escaped.

I dropped my paintbrush and closed my arms around her. I'd wanted her to come to me, to freely choose me because I was worthy of that choice. But I couldn't stand there and let her cry. "I made a mistake, see. A huge one." She was permitting the embrace but not hugging me back, just standing there with her hands over her face while my arms encircled her. "Everything about Saturday was perfect," I said, moving my lips against her hair. "The painting—the painting I finally got right." I smiled now, to think that Curry's lesson about harnessing emotion had been so simple, so obvious—and yet so impossible for me before Jenny. "The pub—well, the confrontation with Royce I could maybe have done without." She didn't laugh, but she did lean almost imperceptibly closer to me, and I seized the opportunity to tighten my grip on her. "And afterward. In my room." I swallowed. It was scary as hell, but I had to look at her face while I said this, so I pulled back a bit. "I never cared about anything before like I cared about what was happening that night. I never loved anything, or anyone." I swallowed. I didn't want to presume, but it had to be said. "I don't think anyone ever loved me."

"Not even your family? Your mother?"

I was startled to hear her speak. She'd been so still up until now that I'd settled in for a long speech. I shrugged. "She sent me a card at Christmas." When Jenny's lower lip began to quiver, I softened my assessment. "I don't think she ever got over it when my sister ran away." I'd been trying again to just talk, to state my case without touching her. But I couldn't help it. Her hair, which was a complete bird's nest of a mess, was blowing in her face, so I reached out and tucked as much of it as I could behind her ears. "But don't pity me. I didn't consider it any great loss. I was making my way in the world."

"Was?" she whispered.

"Yeah, until you came along with your goddamned cause. And now look at me." I cast a glance over my shoulder and couldn't help smiling even as I rolled my eyes. "What happened to me?"

"I loved you," she whispered. "I think that's what happened."

I'd been trying to make a joke, to make her smile, regardless of what the outcome was going to be, but her words hit me with as much force as if the building demolition had begun and left me buried in the rubble. But I ignored the churning in my chest and nodded. "Yeah." My voice caught, and I cleared my throat, trying again. "And I panicked."

"What do you want?" she asked me. The simple, blunt openness of the question startled me. One thing Jenny had shown me was that you could make yourself vulnerable and not die. Look at her, doing it right now, standing there before a man who'd broken her heart, looking at him with red eyes and tangled hair and asking him a question that meant everything.

"I want to move to New York with you," I said, which was the first and truest answer that popped into my head. "I want you to forgive me. I want you to let me love me." It was the scariest thing I had ever done, but I let the tear I could feel hovering in the corner of my eye spill down my cheek. That I didn't wipe it away, didn't turn my face away from her… I hoped she could recognize these things as the offerings they were. "I want to let you love me…if you want to."

She laughed then, a good laugh, without a hint of bitterness in it. And then she was kissing me but still laughing, so it was a big, sloppy mess. All I could do was try to keep us upright as my arms snaked around her. Relief and lust conspired with each other to make my legs feel like jelly, and I leaned back against the solid mass of the building, grateful for its support.

"Townsend!"

Jenny jumped away from me, as if she'd only just realized we were standing in front of hundreds of people making out as if we were drowning.

Curry stood at the foot of my scaffolding, hands on his hips, apparently done with his "discussion" with the suits. "This is now officially your senior portfolio," he yelled up. "So unless you want to flunk out, I suggest you spend a little less time locking lips with your girlfriend and a little more time getting your ass in gear."

"Are they still going to tear down the building?" Jenny called down.

Curry shrugged as he lit a cigarette. "One miracle at a time, Miss Fields."

"Emmanuel Curry knows my name?" she whispered.

I laughed, and as she tried to pull away from me, I kept hold of her hand.

"What?" She pulled harder on her hand, but still I didn't surrender it. "I'm not going to just sit here and gaze at you adoringly while you paint. I have shit to do."

"What shit?" I said, laughing as I raised her hand to my mouth and pressed an openmouthed kiss to it.

"Well, for one thing, I'm pretty sure I need to brush my hair."

I just raised my eyebrows, because that *was* true.

"And I also need to go pay some attention to my poor, neglected newspaper. Make sure the editor in chief–elect has done a suitable job curating the editorial cartoons for the next edition."

I started to try to say that she didn't have to run that cartoon on my account, but she kept talking over me.

"I also need to go get a new phone number."

I winced. "I'm sorry."

She shrugged. "Eight-six-seven-five-three-oh-nine was overrated." Then she smiled a wicked little Cheshire cat smile. "But I might keep it long enough for you to call me and tell me when you're done here so we can meet up later."

"I'll just come over."

"No way." She swatted my chest. "All those times I called you and left messages that you ignored. I want you to call me back!"

Instead of answering, I lowered my head and kissed her again. This time, no one was laughing. I was dead serious, nudging her lips open with my tongue, stroking her hard and deep. I wanted to mark her, to make her remember what was in store for her once I was done with this goddamned painting.

She sighed into my mouth and sagged against me, all soft curves and rainbows.

The thought came back. It had never left, really. But this time, I could think it without fear, confident that it was the simple, powerful truth that would change the rest of my life.

I was made to kiss Jenny Fields.

EPILOGUE

One year later.

MATTHEW

When the pebbles hit the window, I knew I was in trouble. There had been no pebbles for a good three weeks now, so I thought I had made my point.

I heaved open the sticky, ancient window in our microscopic living room and leaned out.

"Hi!" Jenny called up. She was dressed in her pink hoodie and, standing next to the graffiti-covered (and not the good kind of graffiti—the "artist" clearly had very little respect for his medium) Laundromat at the foot of our Avenue A walk-up, she looked like a happy flamingo in a war zone. It had been a little over a year since we'd arrived in New York, and my breath still caught when I saw her like this, all vibrant in the face of the gritty, unforgiving city.

She also had a piece of furniture—a oddly shaped shelf thing—next to her.

"Whatever that is, it's not coming up unless something else goes," I said, even though I knew it was futile.

Jenny worked in the classified department at the *New York Daily News*. According to her, it was a shitty entry-level job, though the assignment desk had started letting her write the occasional low-level obituary and once, when there was no one else around, they'd sent her to cover the opening of a mall in Queens. The only perk of the classifieds gig, she said, was that hers was the first set of eyeballs on each ad, so she could cherry pick "the good stuff" for us—which was pretty much how we had furnished our tiny fifth-floor apartment.

And furnished it some more. And some more.

But three weeks ago, when a stack of Culture Club cassettes fell off an overpacked shelf and bonked me on the head, I proclaimed that there was no more room at the inn. We struck a deal, in fact. She would stop bringing classifieds stuff home, and I would stop insulting Culture Club.

But there she was, smiling at me from five stories down, and I knew that whatever that shelf-thing was, I would haul it upstairs for her and move shit around until she was happy.

And then I would show her today's mail, and she would be *really* happy.

So I just shook my head, shut the window, and hoofed it down four flights of stairs. When I emerged through the heavy metal door of the building, she was sitting on the aforementioned shelf thing talking to our neighbor: Alejandro Vega by day, "Hairy Debbie" by night in his drag persona. Alejandro and Jenny's shared love of Blondie had made them fast friends, and Jenny dutifully attended every one of Debbie's shows at Pyramid, dressed in her blue bubble dress, which, after years of being mothballed, was now seeing a lot of action.

She was so consistently herself that once you spent any amount of time with her, you wanted more.

I still couldn't believe she'd chosen *me*.

"It's a flat file," she said, springing off her temporary seat and holding her hands up as if to fend off criticism. "The seller was a map collector, but I thought you could use it to store finished paintings. You're always saying how you hate rolling them up. I was thinking that we could move the record player into the bed nook, or even get rid of it. Cassettes are taking over anyway, and—"

I cut her off with a kiss. Just walked right over there, Alejandro and substandard graffiti be damned.

A lump appeared from nowhere in my throat when we separated. I still wasn't accustomed to people caring about me enough to do thoughtful things for me out of the blue. "All right. Let's get this sucker upstairs."

Alejandro helped us wrestle the bulky flat file upstairs, and after he had left, I popped a couple beers, flopped back on the ratty loveseat that was the sum total of our "living room" furniture, and patted the spot next to me.

She sat and took a long pull from the beer I handed her.

"I have something I think you're going to want to read," I said, taking her beer from her and handing her one of the letters that had arrived today.

"Oh my God! It's finally here!

"It's not what you think." She had been waiting on pins and needles for weeks from word from Columbia about whether she would be accepted to the graduate journalism program. "Go on," I said, nodding at it. "I opened it because it was addressed to both of us."

She pulled out the brightly colored flyer, looking at it with the same confusion I had when I'd first opened it. As understanding dawned, a smile blossomed.

"It's from Officer Artie!" she said, turning the paper to me so I could see the hand-drawn image of the Allenhurst College Art Building—the *newly renovated* Allenhurst College Art Building, to be more precise. Below the picture, it said, "Grand Re-Opening Reception" and gave some information about where and when. Artie had written a note in the margin.

Word on the street is that the "troublemakers" who saved this building aren't being invited to its grand re-opening. But were they to somehow find out about it, the administration has been assured that the Allenhurst Campus Police Service has recently updated its riot gear.

"Eeeee!" she screamed. "I almost couldn't believe it when they said they were going to reno instead of demo."

"Looks like it's a done deal," I said, grinning because her enthusiasm was, as always, infectious.

"You did it!" she said.

"No, *you* did it," I said.

"*We* did it." She waved the flyer back and forth. "Anyway, can we go?"

"Of course. We just need to make sure it doesn't conflict with anything."

"What could be more important? I'll take a vacation day, and they won't give you any trouble at the store, will they?" I shook my head. I was working at an art supply store, which, in addition to providing me with a discount on supplies, had helped me get in with a community of artists, including my boss, a cool woman who was great about accommodating her staff members' schedules.

"I mean, I guess if you sold a painting," Jenny said, "and, like, the buyer had to see you on that day." Curry had put me in touch with some gallery owners in the city, and a couple of them were showing some of my stuff. No sales yet, but I had faith that they would come. Well, Jenny had faith—enough for us both.

"Yeah," she went on. "Selling a painting would be the only excuse I would accept. Otherwise, nothing is keeping us from this re-opening."

"Well, nothing, except you'll want to make sure you don't have any conflicting commitments"—I produced the second letter I'd been hiding—"involving Columbia."

"Oh my God, it *is* here!" She punched my shoulder before scrambling for the letter. My heart thudded as I watched her open it. I was almost certain she was going to get in, but I also knew she was going to be okay regardless of what that letter said. Jenny was going to be a journalist no matter what. Hell, she already was. I smiled to myself because in this case, the tables were turned. *I* had enough faith in that fact for both of us.

"Ahhh!" The Columbia shriek was louder than the Officer Artie shriek. But then she burst into tears. I was stunned. What the hell was wrong with Columbia?

But then, just was I was about to wrap my arms around her, she whispered, "I got in. And I got a scholarship."

That was more like it. I was so proud of her, I wanted to bust.

She climbed onto my lap and threw her arms around me. I tried to shift her a little. She was basically straddling me, and my body was having its typical reaction to her proximity. I didn't want to mar her victory with a boner. It seemed wrong, somehow.

But she wiggled until she was back on top of my poor cock. "Let's celebrate."

"What did you have in mind?" I said, getting a sense of what kind of party she was talking about.

"Hmmmm." She performed an exaggerated shrug. "I don't know. Maybe we should go out and do some graffiti?"

"Nah." I hadn't done a graffiti run since college. I was busy with work and painting. But also, I just didn't feel the need anymore. It was like Jenny and Curry had unlocked something inside me. I wasn't happy all the time —this wasn't a fairy tale, after all—but I was able to use my art to get the same sense of relief that graffiti used to give me.

It was my turn to tease her. "I bet you want to call your dad." But as I said it, I ground myself against her, relishing the little whimper I got in return.

"I don't think so," she said, nuzzling my neck. I was proud of the way she was handling her dad. It wasn't easy, but she'd reached out to a few of his neighbors and told them about the situation. They looked in on him from time to time, so the burden wasn't hers alone anymore.

I unzipped her hoodie and snaked my hands under the hem of the shirt she wore beneath it. "Well, crap, I'm out of ideas. I guess your triumph will just have to go uncelebrated."

Laughing, she levered herself off me. Well, she tried to, but I held tight.

"Let me go!" The wriggling she did as she tried to escape my clutches pretty much ensured that I would not be obeying that particular directive.

But then she said the one thing guaranteed to get me to do her bidding. "I just need to run to the bathroom and grab my sponge."

I threw my hands in the air like I was being robbed, and she laughed harder.

"Stay there," she said, pointing at me and trying to look stern. "Don't go anywhere, okay?"

I grinned. "You got it, Rainbow Brite."

ACKNOWLEDGMENTS

A super-duper enormous shout out to my friend Audra North. Audra organized the anthology that this story first appeared in, *'80s Mix Tape: A Romance Rewind Anthology*. The New Wave Newsroom Series would not exist without her. What I thought was going to be a fun, nostalgic one-off ended up being book one in a new series, which I decided to make my first foray into independent publishing. Audra had invaluable feedback at every step in this process, starting way back when I was first imagining the characters and extending to explaining pretty much every aspect of indie publishing to me.

My agent, Courtney Miller-Callihan, provided great feedback on the first draft of this story, even though she wasn't going to get to sell it. If that isn't a full-service agent, I don't know what is.

Gwen Hayes, fellow daughter of the 1980s, improved this book immensely. Her comments helped shape this book, and reading her own totally tubular contribution to the original anthology really helped get me in the mind-set.

My oldest writing friends, Erika Olbricht and Sandra Owens, provided commentary on an early draft, and, as always, much-needed cheerleading.

Copy editor extraordinaire Polly Watson saved me from myself about a billion times.

Michele Harvey helped me figure out how common telephones would be in the dorm rooms of the era.

This was my maiden voyage into the uncharted seas of independent publishing, and boy, oh, boy was the learning curve steep! I benefitted immensely from advice from many writing friends, particularly Audra North, Sandra Owens, Zoe York, Deborah Cooke, and Melanie Card. Thank you for being so generous with your expertise.

Dani and Jasmyn at Barclay Publicity were an enormous help in helping me get this newbie indie effort off the ground.

Finally, I have to tip my hat to Tommy Tutone. All the books in the New Wave Newsroom series are inspired by a single song from the 1980s (not necessarily a New Wave song, if you're gonna get technical… But I'm not gonna get technical). This book's inspiration was, of course, "Jenny/867-5309." (I wasn't actually naming the main character after myself, y'all.)

CONNECT WITH ME

Sign up for my newsletter at jennyholiday.com/newsletter. I send newsletters when I have a new release or a sale, and I sometimes include giveaways and access to freebies only for subscribers. Or you can find me on Twitter at @jenny-holi or Instagram at @holymolyjennyholi. (I'm technically on Facebook, but I'm rarely actually there.) Visit my website at jennyholiday.com.

Reviews really help authors, not only because they help us find new readers but because more reviews means more favorable treatment by retailers' algorithms. If you're moved to leave an honest review of this book or any of my others on the retailer's site where you bought it, I'd be most grateful.

ABOUT THE AUTHOR

Jenny Holiday started writing at age nine when her awesome fourth grade teacher gave her a notebook and told her to start writing some stories. That first batch featured mass murderers on the loose, alien invasions, and hauntings. (Looking back, she's amazed no one sent her to a kid-shrink.) She's been writing ever since. After a detour to get a PhD in geography, she worked as a professional writer for many years. Later, her tastes having evolved from alien invasions to happily-ever-afters, she tried her hand at romance. Today she is a USA Today bestselling author of all sorts of romance novels: contemporary and historical, straight and gay. She lives in London, Ontario.

www.jennyholiday.com
jenny@jennyholiday.com
Twitter: @jennyholi
Instagram: @holymolyjennyholi
Newsletter: jennyholiday.com/newsletter

BOOKS BY JENNY HOLIDAY

AN EXCERPT FROM THE GOSSIP

NEW WAVE NEWSROOM #2

September 1980

Chapter One

DAWN

It wasn't like I was actually doing anything wrong. I was just *standing* there. Is it my fault that "there" happened to be the parking lot of the strip mall that was home to Allenhurst Discount Liquors? The last time I checked, it was a free country. I'm allowed to stand in a parking lot. And anyway, how did the campus cop who came swooping in like he was Clint Eastwood escaping from Alcatraz know that I wasn't standing there killing time until my appointment for a fitting at Hearing Aid Depot? Or contemplating a purchase at Billy's Bait and Tackle?

"Because these guys walked out of the liquor store and made their way directly to you, whereupon I observed them hand you a brown paper bag. Then I observed you hand them a wad of cash," said the hulking cop, who was apparently intent on ruining my Alpha Phi rush week assignment, which was to procure six bottles of vodka for tonight's party at Delta Chi, Alpha Phi's brother frat.

I had to get into Alpha Phi. *Had* to. It was the best sorority on campus—it was the best sorority in the *nation*—and it would guarantee that I'd be at the top of the social pyramid at this school. This wasn't high school. If I wanted to be a big fish at Allenhurst College, being an Alpha Phi sister was a sure-fire shortcut. And let's face it, if I wasn't popular, I wasn't anything. I wasn't too proud to admit that to myself. My looks were only okay, though I could rock some bitchin' bangs and was known for my elaborate, multicolored eye shadow designs. I wasn't hugely smart—I only got into Allenhurst College because my father went here and he donates buckets of money to them. So popularity was what I had to work with.

I had done a ton of research the summer before coming here and had decided that Alpha Phi was my ticket to social status. I wasn't even looking to get a bid anywhere else and had focused all my rush week efforts on impressing the sisters. Besides, I had already done all the sisters' eye makeup for tonight—and there were *fifty-two* of them. That was a lot of effort already invested, and I'd be damned if Officer Unfriendly here was going to tank my chances.

I sized him up, trying to figure out how to play this. He was looking at my driver's license while the two Delta Chi juniors I'd sweet-talked into buying for me produced theirs for another officer. My officer was built, I'll say that much about him—much more so than the one dealing with the guys. Muscular arms strained against his blue button-down cop shirt like they could barely be contained. A trim waist topped off a pair of legs encased in navy blue cargo pants tucked into a pair of black combat boots. He had close-cropped black hair, and he was frowning. He reminded me a little of a younger Erik Estrada from *CHiPS*, except Officer Ponch was always smiling, whereas this guy looked like he was sucking on a Sour Patch Kid. It was hard to really get a read on him, though, because a pair of mirrored aviator sunglasses obscured his eyes.

I made an exaggerated sniff, which drew his attention. "Officer"—I glanced at his name tag—"Perez, I'm really sorry." I put on my best puppy-dog face. "I guess I got carried away with the idea of being in college. It's the end of the first week of classes, you know, and I was feeling a little homesick, so a few of us were going to have a little get-together."

"A little get-together?" His tone was incredulous, and I could imagine him raising his eyebrows behind those glasses even though I couldn't see it happening. When I didn't answer right away, he said, "You're buying for the Delta Chi party tonight.

That isn't a 'little gathering.'"

"I am not! I—"

"Forget it, Dawn," said one of the frat guys. "Officer Perez knows everything about Allenhurst College. There's no escaping him once you're in his clutches."

I shivered a little at that notion but shook it off. Well, okay, maybe I wasn't getting that vodka, but that didn't mean I couldn't manage the fallout from the situation. Because Officer Perez was starting to look like maybe he wasn't going to be satisfied with merely issuing a warning.

I manufactured a louder sniff. This one drew everyone's attention: the two frat guys, Officer Perez, and his partner all turned to me. I noted that Officer Unfriendly and his sidekick were wearing different uniforms, a fact I filed away for later. Right now, I had to follow up on that sniff.

"You aren't going to call my parents, are you?" Never mind that I only had one, and that Daddy finding out I was drinking probably wouldn't even rate a phone call. I stuck out my lower lip and tried to make it quiver, not enough that I could be accused of purposeful manipulation, but enough—I hoped—that I was communicating some remorse.

"Nope," said Officer Perez, totally unaffected by my emotional display. "You're eighteen. Welcome to adulthood."

"Welcome to adulthood, yet I'm not allowed to buy alcohol?"

"That is correct." He handed my ID to the cop next to him, and that cop flipped open a little notepad and started writing on it.

"You're a campus cop," I said, letting my gaze rake over Perez's belt. It held a baton and handcuffs and a few other things I didn't recognize, but no gun. The other guy had a gun. And there was the difference in the uniforms I'd noticed earlier.

He glanced at the patch on his right biceps that read ALLENHURST COLLEGE PD. It was stretched taut over the muscle. "And you have a talent for stating the obvious."

"Do you even have jurisdiction here? Because we're not actually on campus." We were a mere two blocks from it, but still. If he wasn't going to respond to my remorseful-little-girl act, maybe I could wiggle out through a procedural loophole.

"That's why this guy"—he jerked his thumb at the

colleague I'd come to think of as Good Cop—"is writing your ticket."

"Teamwork," Good Cop said, smiling as he ripped off the ticket and held it out to me. "Allenhurst PD at your service, miss."

"Oh, so you need a real cop to close your deals." I was being a brat for no reason now, but I hated the fact that this big guy, this big *gunless* guy, could just step in and ruin everything.

The big gunless guy in question took a step toward me. God, he *was* big. Maybe he didn't need a gun because of those tree-trunk arms. They looked like they were more than sufficient to take on any villain. "Perhaps you'd prefer that instead of issuing you that fifty-dollar possession ticket, I have my 'real cop' friend here arrest you," he said. "And hey, while we're at it, we'll get your friends for furnishing alcohol to a minor."

"You can't do that!"

He took another step, leaving only a few inches between us. My eyes were level with the middle of his chest, so I had to crank my neck back to maintain eye contact. He was probably doing it on purpose, trying to intimidate me and compensate for his lack of a gun.

He smirked. "Perhaps you'd care to add resisting arrest?"

Ugh! What a dickweed! The last thing I needed was to get the Delta Chi guys in trouble. That would hurt my Alpha Phi chances more than anything. So I took a step back—grudgingly. "No...sir."

I wasn't sure why I added the "sir," but something flared in his eyes when I said it, and he took the ticket from the other cop and held it out. I extended my hand, and instead of letting go of the paper once I had hold of it, he pressed it into my palm and used his hand to close my fingers over it. Then he used his other hand to cradle mine, which resulted in him holding my closed fist between his hands like it was the filling in a hand sandwich. It was the kind of gesture you'd make if you were giving someone something really important, like a lost heirloom or, I don't know, the keys to the kingdom. Not a ticket for underage drinking.

His hands were—of course—huge. They engulfed my fist. It occurred to me, with a jolt, that these were the hands of a man. I'd had boyfriends in high school, but looking at Officer Unfriendly's behemoth chest and feeling his warm, callused hands totally surrounding mine made me feel like the emphasis with past boyfriends had been on the *boy* part.

I'd been unknowingly holding my breath, which was stupid, because when I remedied that fact, the resultant inhale came out sounding perilously close to a gasp.

Officer Unfriendly dropped my hands and pressed his lips together as if the stick up his ass were being shoved even higher. "Welcome to college, Miss Hathaway."

AN EXCERPT FROM FAMOUS

FAMOUS #1

Seven years ago

Sometimes a wedding was not just a wedding.

This one, in which Evan Winslow's friend Tyrone pledged his eternal devotion to his girlfriend Vicky, was, in fact, a test. It looked like a normal wedding, with white funereal-looking flowers and ill-fitting tuxedos, but it was *also* Evan's Hail Mary pass: one last attempt to hold on to his life in Miami, to his nascent career, to his entire freaking life.

His final experiment to measure how extensive—how *permanent*—the damage inflicted by his father on the Winslow family's reputation was going to be.

Evan had laid low for the past two weeks, hoping the whole "out of sight/out of mind" adage would prove true, and now it was final exam time.

This test had one question: Could Evan attend his friend Tyrone's wedding and not be recognized, not upstage the proceedings with his mere presence?

The answer was no. Fail. Flunk.

Which meant this was it. Today was the end of life as

he knew it, which sounded melodramatic but was no less true for it. Because if Evan knew one thing with certainty, down to the dusty corners of his soul, it was that he could not live with the fame—the *infamy*—his father's crimes had brought down on his head. He had already been coming around to accepting the idea that his painting career was done before it had even really started—thanks to the crimes of Evan Winslow Sr., Evan Winslow Jr. was destined to be persona non grata in the art world—but now he'd brought the goddamned paparazzi to his best friend's wedding.

He'd tried to hedge against that prospect, and he initially thought he'd succeeded. He'd spent the night at his brother's place. Evan's brother wasn't in the art world—the family business—having opted instead for life as an overgrown trust-fund baby. So he wasn't getting as much media attention as Evan. Evan had called a cab to his brother's house, timing things so as to arrive at the church just before the ceremony started.

But he'd miscalculated, emerging from the taxi as a limo pulled up and disgorged the bride and her attendants.

He'd held out a shred of hope that the flashbulbs that started going off were actually for the bride. But how many brides hired half a dozen photographers with zoom lenses to photograph their nuptials?

How many wedding photographers yelled things like "Were you in on it too?" and "Will you attend the sentencing hearing?"

So he'd hustled inside ahead of the bridal party and tried to make himself inconspicuous.

Which, of course, had set off a series of whispers among the guests. People talking behind wedding programs, some openly pointing at him. The bride's mother glaring, no doubt because he had upstaged her daughter before she'd even made an appearance.

It didn't even matter that everyone recognized him, really. The fact that he had failed his test was regrettable but not elementally important. Because even if the infamy died down, could he live with the lie? With the notion that everything he had—his luxe condo; his painting ability, honed over years of lessons from the world's greatest artists; his expensive grad school—was all built on lies and paid for with stolen money?

The answer to that question was also no.

So it was time to go. To start over somewhere else. Pack his shit up, transfer to another college to finish his degree—say goodbye to his entire life.

He had no earthly idea how to do that, but that was a problem to be solved tomorrow, on day one of his new life. Right now, the last day in his old life, he had a wedding to attend.

Thankfully, the music changed at that moment, signaling the start of the ceremony. Everyone turned, and he breathed a sigh of relief. For a few moments anyway, there were people in the room who would attract more attention than he would.

He almost laughed as the first bridesmaid appeared. The dress was ridiculous. She looked like a short, puffy, pink mummy. Evan didn't know fabrics, but he suspected that the multi-layered, shiny dress she was wearing had not been constructed from any fiber or dye that occurred naturally in this world.

And there was another one, and another. They kept coming, parading down the aisle in ascending order of height, like caricatures of bridesmaids rather than actual bridesmaids, with their identical upswept hairdos and identical pink heels.

His wrist twitched. They would make a great painting, all of them lined up like nesting dolls.

No, correction: as the final bridesmaid appeared at the top of the aisle, Evan had to revise his previous thought. They would make a great painting, but *she* would make a spectacular painting. He would title it *Bridesmaid Number Seven*.

Tall and thin with long limbs, she was the sort of person people might describe as gangly. It was like someone had taken a regular, average woman and stretched her out like taffy. But she was too graceful to be rightfully called gangly. She had an ease about her, which was rather remarkable, given the packaging and spackling she'd been subjected to.

Evan noticed those sorts of details when a painting was emerging. It was like his brain clicked into some other mode as it swept over a scene, processing, neutrally assessing everything with equal attention, waiting for the jolting spike of feeling that signified the correct take on a subject.

He was a beat behind everyone else standing for the bride because he was still looking at the last bridesmaid. She and her colleagues arrayed themselves at the front of the church and turned to watch the bride process. Her face had interesting angles: sharp cheekbones and slightly unruly brows arching high over eyes that should have been too close-set to be called pretty.

Where would he put her? In a forest, maybe? In her ridiculous pink dress in a forest, Titania styled by Barbie? No. That wasn't quite right.

As the bride passed his pew, he forced his gaze from

her tallest attendant and considered his friend Tyrone's soon-to-be-wife with more attention than he had ever found it necessary to bestow on her before. Vicky had the same facial structure as the bridesmaid, but less of it. The cheekbones were there, just not as prominent. The two women had to be related. Sisters, maybe?

As Vicky's father kissed her and sat down, the bridesmaids turned their backs to the congregation, presenting the assembly with a row of identical bows on their backsides, each one a little higher than the one next to it thanks to the arrangement of attendants from shortest to tallest.

He was still thinking about her face, though.

He would start with Yellow Ochre and add tiny amounts of Cadmium Red Light to start with, and then he'd layer in the planes of those gorgeous cheekbones.

It was with a jolt, a great wrenching, invisible blow, that he realized: *no.*

Not that those were the wrong colors, but that he wasn't going to paint her.

He wasn't going to paint anything.

After today, he didn't paint anymore.

* * *

"Is that cute guy in the corner the son of the infamous art criminal?" Emmy whispered to her cousin Vicky. Now that dinner and the first dance were over, she'd finally gotten a minute alone with the bride so she could ask about the handsome man sitting alone at a table in the back of the ballroom. She figured he must be "the one" since she'd seen him intently speed walking past a clump of photographers before they went into the church.

He'd been staring at her much of the evening.

It started when she was walking back up the aisle after the ceremony on the arm of her assigned groomsman. The intensity of his gaze had drawn her attention, but he'd looked away when she caught him staring.

And she'd *kept* catching him. His appraisal had continued throughout the toasts and as she'd tried to make conversation with the rest of the wedding party over dinner. She'd glance over at him only to find him already looking at her—enough times that he'd started grinning sheepishly, like he knew he'd been busted.

But of course if she kept catching him, it meant *she* was staring at *him* as much as he was staring at her.

It was just so hard *not* to look at him. He was tall and broad-shouldered under his impeccably tailored suit, and when he smiled as she'd catch him looking, he did it with his whole face.

"Don't look!" Emmy shriek-whispered as Vicky turned to peek over her shoulder.

"I can't tell you who he is if I can't see him," Vicky declared, not even trying to make her surveillance subtle. "Oh! Yep, that's Evan Winslow!"

"His dad even made the papers in Minnesota," Emmy said. The story of the jet-setting art dealer's fall from grace had all the makings of a Greek tragedy, and it was playing out in the tabloids. It was a true-crime story that had the nation fascinated, except instead of dead bodies there were Ponzi schemes and counterfeit art.

"Yep," said Vicky. "The trial was huge. They were one of the richest families in Miami. It's been all over the place. Poor guy. Ty says he's taken it all super hard." She cocked her head. "So you think he's cute, huh? A little nerdy for my tastes, but I dare you to go over there and talk to him."

"No way! I can't just—" Emmy's objection was cut off when the DJ cued up a horrid song that made Vicky's sorority sisters scream and rise as one.

As they swept Vicky away in a tornado of pink tulle, she called, "Go over there. What have you got to lose? You'll never see him again anyway."

There was so much more she wanted to ask Vicky. How old was Evan Winslow? What was he studying? Vicky's new husband knew him from the University of Miami, where they were both grad students. Tyrone was doing his MBA, but she had a hard time imagining this guy in a business school. He seemed like more of an intellectual—a humanities type maybe. His hair, though currently slicked back, seemed like it was a little too long for him to fit in with the would-be capitalists, and his nerd-chic horn-rimmed glasses seemed more Buddy Holly than business. She started to make up a story. Something from the point of view of a sensitive guy forced into business school by his conniving, greedy father. The chorus could be the dad talking, but by the end of the song, the lyrics would be turned around, the guy defiantly using the father's words against him.

Well, hell. Emmy wasn't generally an assertive sort of person. She tended to hang around on the sidelines and make up little snippets of songs about what she saw unfolding around her. But Vicky was right. She was flying back to Minneapolis tomorrow, and she'd never see this guy again. In twenty-four hours, she'd be back doing battle with her parents, facing their perpetual and poorly disguised disappointment over her barista job and her "childish dreams." So why not put an end to their little mutual staring society and go say hi to the infamous Evan Winslow?

Gathering about a thousand yards of pink polyester in her arms, she hiked up her skirts and set off. He must have felt her approach, because he looked up from his cake while she was still a good twenty feet away, an expression of surprise seguing into another of those magnetic, self-deprecating grins as she got closer.

"Hey," she said, trying to make the greeting seem casual.

"Hey," he echoed. Then he added, "You're here," as if all this time he'd merely been waiting for her arrival, as if *she* had been the point of his attending the wedding.

He picked up a wedding program and slid it across the table to her.

"Ha!" She laughed in delight. If she'd been making up a story about him, it seemed he had done the same thing, in a way. Except where hers was coming together from turns of phrase and snippets of melody, his was composed of ink—garden-variety ballpoint from the look of it. He had drawn her on the back of the program, right on top of the Shakespeare sonnet that Vicky, who Emmy was pretty sure wouldn't know a sonnet if it bit her in the ass outside the context of wedding planning websites, had artfully placed on the otherwise-blank heavy-gauge paper. The funny thing was that Emmy wasn't wearing the god-awful dress in his portrait. He'd put her in shorts and a tank top, which was pretty much her uniform when she wasn't performing bridesmaid duties.

"You drew me! You're an artist?" She'd known his dad was an art dealer, but she didn't know that much about the rest of the Winslow family—she'd read the headlines but hadn't really followed the details of the trial.

He paused for long enough before answering that she started to fear she'd offended him somehow. "I used to be a painter."

"What does that mean?"

"It means I used to paint, but now I don't."

Okay then, that was clearly not a topic he was keen to discuss, so she tried another question. "Vicky said you're in grad school with Tyrone?"

"We're both at the University of Miami, but I'm doing a PhD in art history. Ty and I met in a campus running club."

Yes. The satisfying ping of having uncovered the truth in her proto-song echoed in her chest. An artist *and* an intellectual. She'd been spot-on.

"Are you from Minnesota?" he asked. "You look like you're related to Vicky."

"Yeah. She's my cousin. I'm Emmy."

He stood and stuck out his hand. "Hi, Emmy. I'm Evan."

She was on the other side of the table—too far away to reach his hand—so she walked around. Wanting to pretend that she was in control, she slowed her steps. But that was only because she wasn't entirely comfortable with the truth of the matter, which was that in her haste to reach him she'd *had* to slow her steps. She was a stupid, powerless fish he was reeling in.

He didn't let go when the handshake would normally have ended, just hitched his head toward the door. "Want to go for a walk?"

Of course she did.

* * *

"Aha!" Evan said, pushing his shoulder against the heavy metal door at the top of the stairwell. "Unlocked!" He held it for a laughing Emmy to precede him onto the roof of the banquet hall. She had her voluminous skirts gathered in one hand and her high heels dangling from the fingers of the other. "Be careful of your feet. Who knows what's up here."

She paused at the threshold and peered out. He looked over her shoulder. Yeah, the gravel that lined the ground was going to require shoes. Or...

"Eeee!" she shrieked, laughing as he swung her into his arms. "What are you doing?"

What *was* he doing? He was acting like the hero of some lame made-for-TV romantic comedy. Not his style at all. But there was something about being in limbo, teetering on the precipice between one life and another, that made every decision this evening seem less important, every action less imbued with its potential future consequences.

"If I'd known that 'go for a walk' was code for 'break onto the roof,'" she said, "I might have thought twice about accompanying you."

The roof had been the only place he could think to escape, where he could be sure there would be no photographers. But he didn't want her to feel uncomfortable, so he paused, wondering if he should turn around.

But then she craned her neck to get a better view and said, "It's gorgeous up here!"

So he crossed the roof and deposited her on some kind of ventilation structure that would do as a bench.

"Beautiful," she said, still talking about the view.

It was. The buildings of the Miami skyline he knew so

well were jewels against the otherworldly pink sky of dusk. But so were the shining sapphires of her eyes.

And that was another made-for-TV thing he didn't do: compare women's eyes to gemstones. *What the hell?* There was limbo, and there was losing control of himself.

"Give me that," she said, grabbing the stolen bottle of champagne he had tucked under his arm and setting to work on the cork. When it popped, she squealed and held the fizzing bottle away from her for a moment before tipping her head back and drinking directly from it. The slanted pink light caught tendrils of blond hair escaping the pins that anchored an elaborate updo. He watched her throat undulate as she drank. Then she lifted her head, used her forearm to wipe her mouth, and grinned as she handed him the bottle, perfectly framed by the blazing sunset.

He was cursed with a painter's eye. He saw things other people didn't. He was never going to get over not painting her.

"What's your last name?" he asked, thinking, irrationally, that if he knew it, he could somehow find her later. Put a bookmark in this meeting and come back to it, even though he knew that he was going to have to draw a sharp line between what he was already starting to think of as his "old" life and whatever was going to come next.

"I'm moving to Los Angeles in two months," she said.

"So it's Emmy I'mMovingToLosAngelesInTwoM-onths?" He couldn't help teasing. "That must have been a mouthful when you were a kid."

"No." She laughed. "I'm moving in two months, and I'm going to change my name when I do, I think. I haven't decided to what. So it's just Emmy for now."

Ah, so he wasn't the only one on the verge of reinventing himself. Perhaps that's why he felt this strangely, strongly compelled by her. They were of a kind. "If that's how you're going to be, I won't tell you my last name, either." She likely already knew it, but she hadn't brought it up, so he wouldn't either.

"Don't tell me," she said. "Let's just be Emmy and Evan. E and E." She took another swig of the champagne. "Like e.e. cummings."

"I will wade out till my thighs are steeped in burning flowers," he said. He wasn't sure how his brain had produced that obscure line, but he knew now how he would have painted her.

She'd been looking at the skyline, but the cummings snippet snagged her attention, and she turned, eyes suddenly glazed with moisture.

"What's the matter?"

"I'm a songwriter," she said. "Or at least I'm trying to be."

Ah. The impending move to L.A., the name change—the pieces were coming together.

"Sometimes when I hear a line like that, it makes me despair of ever writing anything worthwhile," she said, shaking her head.

"Don't despair. You can do it."

"How do you know? You don't even know me."

He shrugged. She had intelligent eyes that looked intently at the world. That's what storytellers needed. That's probably what he had seen in her, why he had picked her out from the row of identical puffy pink dresses. "I have a feeling you're going to make it."

"You're the only one who thinks so," she whispered.

"I have a good eye," he said, struck with the urge to reassure her. "I see things other people don't." He turned so they were side by side, both facing the now rapidly darkening city—which was why he didn't have any warning when she leaned over, grabbed his cheeks, and kissed him.

Her lips were soft, and pressed so lightly against his it almost tickled. His first instinct was to push her away, because what could come of it? They were both headed for new lives, both making a break with the present.

But he couldn't make himself do it. What was so wrong with kissing a pretty girl on a rooftop? It was the perfect coda, actually, to his Miami life. So he surrendered, letting his whole body relax into the soft hunger of their kiss, forcing himself to attend to every nuance of the experience, to savor the bittersweet finale, as if he could file it away somehow, and take it out and examine it again later, like he would a memento from his past.

And, oh, he hadn't felt this alive for months. It was like she was filling him with energy he thought had been drained permanently by the police raids, the meetings with lawyers and PR people, the endless court proceedings. He sipped at her lips, letting his hands frame her face, wanting to anchor her there forever. As he deepened the kiss, testing the seam of her lips, she opened for him, but there was a tentativeness there, a hesitation.

It was like she didn't really know what she was doing.

The rogue thought entered his mind as her tongue slid along his, ripping an involuntary groan from his throat as he gently pushed her away.

"How old are you?" God, how could he have missed that? Hadn't he just been bragging about how good he was at seeing things?

Her brow furrowed. "Does it matter?" She was flushed, her pupils dilated, her breath short.

She was gorgeous.

It didn't matter how old she was, not in any elemental way. But it *did* matter here on this roof, in the clumsy corporeal world. It meant the difference between continuing this spectacular goodbye-to-his-old-life kiss and *not* continuing it.

"Tell me."

She pulled back and scooted farther away from him on the bench, confirming his fears even before she spoke. "I'm nineteen."

Right. It might be perfectly clear that this was merely a casual kiss, but he wasn't going to be *that* guy. He eyed the nearly empty champagne bottle on the ground at their feet. That was all he needed—the story of Evan Winslow, Jr. getting a nineteen-year-old drunk and seducing her.

So much for enjoying his bittersweet Miami coda.

"How old are *you?*" she countered, a challenge in her voice.

"Twenty-six."

"That's not so bad," she said.

"Not so bad for what?" He was teasing her, but only because teasing was all he could do now. "You're right," he said. "A seven-year age difference is not bad at all for sitting on the roof talking about everything under the sun until someone notices we're gone and sends out a search party." He patted the seat beside him, shrugged out of his suit jacket, and held it out to her.

He wasn't a *total* saint, though. He liked the disappointment that washed across the striking angular face he wanted to paint so bad his fingers ached.

"Talking," she said, pouting a little but sliding back over to sit next to him and letting him slip the jacket over her shoulders.

"*Talking*," he confirmed, emphasizing the word for himself as much as for her.

"Okay, uh, what's your favorite TV show?"

"I don't really watch TV." He didn't tell her that he didn't even own one. Or that the glimpses of his family's sordid drama that he'd caught on CNN at his brother's house had been enough to reinforce his desire to never get one.

"Last concert you saw?"

He thought—hard—and came up with nothing. He had been to a few shows on the last cruise he took with his parents. His mother dragged Evan and his brother and their father on an annual luxury cruise and made them dress for dinner and generally fulfill her fantasy of the perfect Ralph Lauren family. But probably cruise ship bands playing Neil Diamond covers weren't what Emmy had in mind. "I'm not really one for live music," he finally said.

"Okaaay," she said, screwing up her face like she was trying to think of a new topic.

"It's no good," he said laughingly. "I'm completely pop-culturally illiterate."

"How come you don't paint anymore?"

Whoa. If her previous questions had been rubber-tipped darts that pinged easily off their targets, this one was a razor-sharp axe that sliced right through him.

"I don't want to talk about that," he said, which was the absolute truth, even if it didn't answer her question.

"Okay," she said, and he was surprised that she was going to accept his evasive answer. Maybe it wouldn't be so hard to upend his life after all. Maybe he could get used to being not-a-painter. "So what should we talk about?"

"You. We should talk about you." She was the most

compelling person he'd met in a long time. And she was the *only* person he'd met recently who hadn't said a word about his father. "I want to know everything there is to know about you, Emmy NoLastName. Tell me about moving to L.A. Sing me a song." He turned to face her head-on. He would listen to her for as long as he could get away with it. He would listen and watch. Then he would say goodbye.

To her, and to himself.